P9-COO-955

FALLING SHORT

Also by Ernesto Cisneros

Efrén Divided

FALLING

SHORT

Ernesto Cisneros

Quill Tree Books
An Imprint of HarperCollinsPublishers

Quill Tree Books is an imprint of HarperCollins Publishers.

Falling Short
Copyright © 2022 by Ernesto Cisneros
All rights reserved. Printed in Lithuania.
No part of this book may be used or reproduced in any manner
whatsoever without written permission except in the case of
brief quotations embodied in critical articles and reviews. For
information address HarperCollins Children's Books, a division of
HarperCollins Publishers, 195 Broadway, New York, NY 10007.
www.harpercollinschildrens.com

Library of Congress Control Number: 2021949306
ISBN 978-0-06-288172-4

Typography by David DeWitt
21 22 23 24 25 SB 10 9 8 7 6 5 4 3 2 1
❖
First Edition

Dedicated to everyone who has ever felt like they fall short of what the world expects of them

ISAAC

CHAPTER 1

Marco's repeated tapping on my window sounds like Morse code—really, really loud Morse code.

I try to open my eyes, but my left one is being stubborn and refuses to obey. "Go away, Marco!" I say, almost pleading. "Five more minutes."

"Nope. It's our first day of sixth grade at Mendez Middle School. You agreed we should get to school extra early. You were very clear and made me promise to ignore anything you said . . . 'including bribes or threats.'"

Marco's fingertips tap dance against the window. "You know I'm gonna keep going until you get up."

It's not his fault. I did ask for his help.

It's just hard after last night.

I mean, I know that parents sometimes argue. And that it's normal. It's part of life. I get that. But last night, Apa came by to talk with Amá . . . and I had a tough time sleeping through the yelling.

"All right, fine." My left eye finally cooperates. I kick off my sheets and walk over to open the window.

The tip of Marco's nose is squished flat against the glass, almost at eye level with me. This is strange because normally, even on his tiptoes, Marco can barely get his chin past my windowsill.

You know the saying, "Good things come in small packages"? Well, whoever said that was probably talking about Marco. "Fun-sized" is what he likes to call himself, which is way better than being called "adorable," which he gets *a lot*. I wouldn't be surprised if he came home from middle school with bruises on his cheeks from all the older kids—especially the girls—squeezing his face as if he were some sort of stuffed animal.

A word of advice: don't ever do that. He hates it.

Hates hearing how "cute" he is. Unless, of course, you are his dad, who refers to him as his own little "Juju-bean," after the amazing Jujubes candy—on account of Marco being half-Jewish, half-Mexican. Well, at least that's what he *used* to call him, before the divorce.

Anyway, Marco Honeyman is his whole name, and he can't stand getting picked up off the ground and twirled around like a rag doll—something that happened all the time in elementary.

The thing is, he won't say anything about it. He's just wired like that . . . really polite. Really nice. And super responsible. Nothing like me.

I slide the window all the way open. Marco looks wide awake. His hair is slicked and parted, and his shirt is buttoned to the top in Marco fashion. Of course he's ready.

I reach out my hand, offering to help him in, like I usually do most mornings.

Only Marco holds up his hand. "Nope, not today. I got this."

I stand back and watch him leap inside. It's the most athletic thing I've ever seen him do.

Before I can say a word, he leans outside the window and pulls in what looks like a small rolling cooler.

"Whoa, what is that thing?"

Marco shortens the length on the telescoping handlebar and wheels it over to me.

I look closer. *Wait, what?* "Dude, is that a rolling backpack?"

"Not just *any* backpack," he says, patting down the side. "*This* is a ZĪPPA. Not only will it keep me from hurting my back, it doubles as a chair."

"Or a step stool," I say, pretending to step on his ZĪPPA.

"Really? Are you height-shaming me?" Marco says with a gleam of laughter in his eyes. "Because I will leave right now." Immediately, he shoots me a toothy grin.

"That's too bad," I say back, "because I'm starting to smell pancakes and bacon coming from the kitchen. And you know how my Amá is always trying to fatten you up."

Marco scratches his chin and pretends to be thinking the offer through. "Fine," he finally answers. "You're just lucky I don't offend easily."

We both laugh.

"Come on," I say. "Let's eat."

"Sounds good. But, uh . . . maybe you should put some pants on first."

He's right. I *am* getting too old to be running around the house in my underwear.

I go over to my desk chair, reach for the school clothes I picked out last night, and spread my new jeans and favorite Lakers Nation jersey along the side of my bed—the shirt Apá got me at the last game we went to together.

Marco comes over and examines my choice of clothes. "Wow, I'm really impressed." He holds up my boxer-briefs by the waistband. "You even picked out a pair of clean chonies and everything."

"Clean?" I answer, as straight-faced as possible. "What makes you think those are clean?"

He immediately drops them, jokingly wiping his hands along the side of his shirt. "Dude, that's gross."

Amá is in the kitchen, sipping on the same iced coffee she makes at the start of every week, only this morning—after last night—she's drinking it out of an oversized thermos.

"Buenos días, mijos," she says, not at all surprised to see Marco joining us for breakfast. After so many years, it's now kind of expected.

Marco's eyes double in size and he licks his lips at the buffet laid out before us. Fluffy scrambled eggs, bacon, sausage, watermelon scoops, and smiley-faced pancakes stacked high—yup, Amá's definitely gone a bit overboard with breakfast, even for her.

"Wow. Are you expecting company?" Marco asks.

Amá smiles. "Only my favorite visitor."

She leans in and gives him a big squeeze. Marco wraps his arms around her, smiling. My Amá is one of the few adults he gives free passes on hugs.

"See," she says mid-hug, "Marco doesn't mind my hugs. Do you?"

Apparently, she's still bitter after I told her I was too big for hugs now that I'm starting sixth grade. Making sure I get the point, Amá comes close and offers me a straight-arm handshake. I go ahead and lock hands, only her mom instincts prove to be too strong and she pulls me in, squeezing me like I'm an old tube of toothpaste.

"Fine," I say. "You can hug me here at home—just not at school."

Amá crosses herself, promising to try.

I take a seat at the table next to Marco. There's a second plate waiting for me. It's a lot of food, but I'm used to it.

Amá's like that at work too. Always cooking up a feast. When I think about it, I'm not sure she knows how to make a small meal.

If it wasn't for her, our family restaurant, El Comedor Castillo—well . . . back when it used to be one—would have gone under years ago. She works long shifts and does stuff an owner shouldn't be doing. But that's Amá for you. Not too proud to unclog a toilet if needed.

Too bad Apá's contracting job takes so much of his time. She could really use the help.

Amá hands Marco a bottle of ketchup.

"Thank you, Mrs. Castillo."

Amá bites on her lower lip and sighs. "Marco, just so you know, I won't be going by that name any longer. You can call me by my maiden name, Ms. Anguiano . . . or Isaac's mom—that works too."

My heart sinks. Amá's mentioned changing her last name before, but that doesn't make it any easier to hear. She's been pressing Apá to sign the final divorce papers, only he keeps stalling. Keeps telling her that they could work things out. Keeps promising to stop drinking.

"Well, Ms. Anguiano, I promise to remember."

Amá smiles and gives him a second hug. Me, I fight back the urge to fling a pancake at him.

"Hey, Marco," I call out, interrupting the hug, "don't you need to wash your hands before you eat?"

I know I'm acting all semi-aggressive, but I just don't like the idea of Amá and me no longer sharing a last name.

Marco looks down at his hands. "Yeah, I probably should . . . especially after touching your chonies." Isaac's mom crinkles her nose but doesn't ask.

"I'll be right back." He turns to Amá. "Do you mind, Ms. Anguiano?"

"Sweetie, you practically live here. When are you going to stop asking?"

Marco blushes and heads toward the hallway bathroom.

"Que niño tan lindo," says Amá. "Sure hope you meet more friends like him in middle school today."

Suddenly, we hear a screech, which I assume is coming from Abuelita, who moved in with us after Abuelito passed away.

I rush over and find Marco frozen in place just outside the bathroom. Only the screeching is coming from *him*, with his hands over his eyes.

Inside, Abuelita is sitting on the toilet. She seems as alarmed as Marco. Fortunately, her long flannel gown protects my eyes.

"Sorry, Abuelita," I answer back.

"Ay, Dios mío," she answers. "¡Se me olvidó atrancar la puerta!"

She says that every time she forgets to set the

bathroom lock. I close my eyes and shut the door for her.

"¿Amá, otra vez?" my Amá hollers at *her* Amá from the kitchen. "How many times do I need to remind you?"

I'm not sure why Amá gets mad; it's not Abuelita's fault she sometimes forgets. It's just like when I forget my homework on my bed or like when I misplace my cell phone or forget to put on deodorant in the mornings. I don't do these things on purpose either—they just . . . happen.

Guess the apple doesn't fall far from the tree. Apá forgets things too. Mostly small promises, though. Like his promise to help me perfect that Euro-step all those NBA guys are doing. It's pretty much a matter of picking up your dribble, taking a long step, then quickly cutting in another direction. The move looks simple enough. Only it's not. Apá says it's a tough move to master, but I'm not about to let that stop me. Not if I plan on taking my game to the next level.

The thing with Apá, sometimes the promises he breaks are bigger . . . like the one he made to Amá about getting help. Who knows, if Apá can stop drinking, maybe Amá will give him another chance, like she's doing with me this school year.

Amá says middle school is my chance at finally becoming "más responsable," which would mean no more forgetting my lunch, no more missing homework, no more detentions, no more bad grades. And most importantly, no more tears for Amá—at least not because of me.

That's why I asked Marco to come over so early—to guarantee I didn't oversleep and mess things up again. Most of my parents' arguing is centered around me and my low grades. Apá says basketball is teaching me all about discipline and responsibility, while Amá argues it's an added distraction.

It's tough to know who is right. All *I* know is that basketball is the only thing I'm really, really good at. Hopefully, this year, I can change that by getting good grades and finally become the son my parents always wanted, the son they deserve.

And maybe then . . . we can stay a family.

MARCO

CHAPTER 2

Isaac is *so* lucky. His mom makes the best food. Real buttermilk pancakes with deli-cut bacon slices as thick as my pinky fingers. And did I mention the freshly squeezed orange juice? There's so much pulp, it's like biting into a fresh orange. So good.

After stuffing my face with seconds and thirds, I head back home, where a bowl of soggy oatmeal and a burnt slice of toast wait for me. I take a seat at the table and stare down at my plate.

"Let me guess," says Mom, "you ate next door again, right?"

I consider telling her that I didn't, but not only would that mean lying to her, it would also mean having to eat her food. And I'm not really sure my stomach can handle either one.

Somehow Mom seems to know the truth, because she leans in and gives me a squeeze. "Next time, be sure and bring me back a plate."

I nod and give her a kiss on the cheek. I'm lucky my mom isn't bothered by her inability to cook. She says that running her own real-estate agency is *her* way of feeding me.

I check my smartwatch for the weather. My watch predicts an eighty-two-degree day, so I go to my room and trade in my jacket and tie for a simple vest instead.

Isaac's bedroom light is on. I look over to see if he's ready. I'm guessing not by the way he's running around like a madman with a toothbrush dangling from his mouth. *Poor Isaac.* He gets like this whenever things don't go as planned. Like last night.

Even with my window closed, I could hear everything his parents were screaming—including the name-calling.

His dad isn't happy about having to move out *or* the custody arrangement. Said he wants Isaac on weekdays too. But his mom hollered at him about getting help for his drinking and pointed out how lucky he was to be getting Isaac on weekends.

I can't imagine what it's like. No, not the divorce part. I get that. My parents are divorcing too. What I don't get is the whole custody battle thing. *My* dad never bothered fighting over me.

Not that I blame him. I'm not the kind of son you can brag about to all your friends. My dad was a star athlete and the most popular kid at school . . . nothing like me.

Mom tries to make me feel better by pulling out old photo albums and reminding me about the stuff Dad used to do with me. Like when I was little (well . . . littler), and he signed me up for a soccer league during my kindergarten year. Talk about being a disappointment. I spent more time on the ground than I did upright.

I can pretty much picture poor Dad having to stand there, pretending to be proud of me.

The only thing that saved me was having my neighbor and best friend, Isaac, on the same team. At first, I thought he was an "aggressive" because of how fearlessly he played. But he was the only one who ever ran over to help me up anytime I got bumped onto the ground.

Before I knew it, he started sticking up for me. At one point, he even threatened to kick anyone who stole the ball from me.

Too bad even he couldn't do much about the name-calling coming from the sidelines.

No, not the kids—*the parents!* Who would have thought that grown-ups could be even crueler than kids?

I completely understand why my dad stopped going to my games; I completely understand why he stopped coming around altogether, and I completely understand how Isaac must be feeling.

Only I don't want him knowing that I know. I mean, we talk about serious stuff like that all the time. It's kind of our thing. Probably the only thing we have in common.

But I'm not about to bring up what happened last night on our first day of middle school.

Again, I peek over at Isaac's window. No sign of him this time—just the glare coming from the massive MVP basketball trophy beside his bed.

I turn to the trophies in *my* room. Spelling bee champion, Principal's Honor Roll, Top Reader, Times Table Titan, Principal's Choice Award—all geek awards, nothing my dad can brag about.

That's why this year, things are going to change. Don't get me wrong . . . I'm still planning on getting straight As and having perfect attendance. But I'm also going to try out for a sport, something not so physical, something that community kids can play too.

Whatever it is, I hope it makes Dad proud enough to want to show up and cheer me on.

ISAAC

CHAPTER 3

Marco and his mom are parked in my driveway, waiting for me. I rush outside with my backpack swinging wildly at my side. The passenger door automatically slides open.

Marco's mom has the greatest minivan ever! It's got fancy leather seats with built-in butt warmers, a Blu-ray player, and plenty of charging ports for just about any device you could possibly own.

It's like Marco has the coolest things anyone could ask for. I have to admit, I'm a bit jealous.

His van is nothing like ours. We've got a commercial van: full-size *and* white. But it does have metal shelves with heating lamps above them for whenever Amá caters an event. It was Apá's idea—he added them himself. But with business slowing, the lights haven't been used much lately.

I draw in a huge breath, taking in as much of that new-car scent as possible. My mom's got hypoglycemia and needs to be eating all the time, so our van pretty much smells like dried fruit wedges, rolled granola, and those string cheese sticks she lugs around everywhere.

We're about to leave when Amá comes running up to us. "¡Mijo!" she calls out, panting. "You forgot your lunch."

Oh, man. Figures I'd forget something. So much for my fresh start.

I lower my window and act like it's no big deal. Like it's something I can just laugh away. But I can already see the concern on her face. Then again, it might just be disappointment more than anything else.

My stomach tightens. Feels like someone just slugged me in the gut.

Here's the thing: I'm used to messing up. I've been doing that since I started preschool. I'm used to getting lectured about needing to be more responsible. What worries me is what happened last year, at the end of fifth grade, after I missed my nineteenth homework assignment. I tried telling Amá that I had done the assignment, but that I'd left it back at home, on my dresser—but she wasn't having any of it. And yet . . .

She didn't say a word to me in the principal's office.

She didn't say a word to me on the drive home either.

In fact, she didn't say a word to me about it at all. It was like she'd simply given up on me—like she did with Apá.

And that's the part freaking me out right now. I mean, is Amá worried that I'll end up like him?

I would have given anything to hear her lecture me or take away my phone for a week—even a spanking would have been better than just watching her alone on the living room couch, crying . . . waiting for Apá to come home, something we could no longer count on.

No! I refuse to add to her troubles any longer. One way or another, I will be better.

I tuck her lunch into the fold of my arm. "Thanks, Amá."

She smooths down my hair at the top before waving to Marco's mom. "Thank you again for taking the boys to school this week. It really helps me out. It gives me time to get through a pile of invoices for the restaurant."

"De nada." Marco's mom's smile is as contagious as

his. "It's the least I can do to pay you back for all the meals you give Marco. I can't blame him, though. My cooking is pretty bad. Right, Marco?"

Marco's eyes widen. His silence makes everyone laugh. Like I said, he's too nice to ever hurt anyone's feelings.

That's when Amá leans in and gives my forehead a warm peck. My throat swells. I shut my eyes—grateful that Amá appears to be giving me yet another chance. I won't let her down . . . starting now.

Traffic is backed up all the way to the school entrance. We're sitting bumper to bumper, barely moving. Marco lowers his window, sticking his head out like a puppy.

I can already tell there's a different kind of energy at school, one that I really like. Kids are pouring into the school from all directions, by foot, skateboard, bike—even the public electric scooters that Amá won't let me ride.

A few of them are bunched into small circles, talking. Most, though, are just glued to their phones. Back in elementary, we weren't allowed to use our phones, skateboards, or pretty much do anything fun. But that's not all that's different. As we turn into the drop-off area, I don't see any of the kids kissing or hugging their parents goodbye—just as I figured.

In fact, they don't nod, wave, or even look back. Nada.

When our turn approaches, I already have my backpack in hand. I open the door and pretty much tuck-and-roll out of the minivan. The automatic side door shuts behind me as I rush to the sidewalk.

Not Marco. Not only does he lean in and give his mom a long hug, he stands in the middle of the street waving jazz hands, causing traffic to come to a complete stop.

The car behind us honks at him as he adjusts the telescoping handle on his ZĪPPA. Finally, he wheels over next to me, only to have his mom go all paparazzi with her cell phone. "Say cheese!" she calls out.

I cringe-smile as the entire row of cars now honk.

She's like that. It's like she forgets that Marco is way older than he looks.

"All right, Marco," I say, tugging at his arm. "We gotta get our schedule cards."

Marco drags his backpack up the curb, striking me right on the shin. I pull my foot up and rub the spot, but Marco's too busy tucking in his shirt to notice.

"Hey, Marco," I say. "There's no dress code here. You don't need to do that anymore."

"Of course I do. Gotta make a good first impression, right?"

He's right about that. But as I look around, I can't help but notice how no one else has a rolling backpack or tucked-in shirts. "What do you think about carrying your ZÏPPA instead?"

"No way," he answers. "Did you know that kids our age shouldn't carry more than fifteen percent of their own body weight? My binder alone weighs a ton. Besides"—he flicks the handle, sending his backpack spinning like a wooden top—"it practically floats."

I gotta admit, the thing *is* smooth. "Fine. Let's go." I point to a sign posted on the entrance gate with the words *Schedule Pickup* written in thick black letters. "We better look for our classes."

Marco actually looks excited about this—which makes sense . . . for him. It's a pretty safe bet he'll be getting straight As, be MVP of the Academic Pentathlon team, and captain of Speech and Debate.

"This is exciting," says Marco. "Kind of like Christmas, huh?"

Christmas? I hope not. Last Christmas was a total

wreck—as in Apá wrecked the whole holiday. You see, some fathers dress up like Santa Claus and wrap presents for their kids. Not mine. Mine got drunk and passed out in the back seat of his car in some parking lot while Amá and I stayed up, waiting for him.

Marco tugs at his ZÏPPA and smacks a girl right on the anklebone. Poor girl hops on one leg and calls out a few words I've never heard at school. Wow . . . another big difference from elementary.

Excitedly, Marco runs up ahead. I do my best to keep up with him.

After Marco almost trips up half a dozen kids with his rolling backpack, he and I reach the corridor. Hands down, middle school is way busier than elementary. Kids are coming and going in all directions, and we do our best to follow the flow of kids. Earbuds, pimples, and straggly whiskered chins surround me.

Suddenly, someone bumps me. Marco and I look up and see this giant of a boy with a jutted chin and chiseled chest, sporting frosted hair tips. Frostboy walks away oblivious to any contact.

My mind shifts to Marco, to making sure *he's* all right.

But somehow, he's gone!

I scan the flow of kids, searching for Marco. There he is, being pinned against the wall by the crowd. He's tiptoeing, trying his best to maintain eye contact with me. It's weird. I see Marco at home every day. His size—or lack of—never stuck out like this before. Seeing him from a distance, I notice how tiny he really is. If I didn't know him, I'd guess he was still in elementary—fourth grade, tops!

I lock my elbows firmly ahead of me and push my way through the crowd until I reach him.

Marco looks back at me all bug-eyed. "Oh my God . . . these kids. They're huge, like sharks!"

I laugh. Here's the thing about Marco. He likes to categorize kids the same way they do fish at the pet store down our block. Marco's theory is simple:

First, you've got the aggressive kids—total bettas that don't get along with others and are very likely to go seek out smaller fish to feast on.

Then you got yourself the semi-aggressives, who can coexist with others, as long as they are of the same size and personality. But under the right conditions, they've been known to eat smaller fish too.

Finally, we get to community fish, a class of non-aggressives who get along with everyone—regardless of type, color, or size. This is how Marco sees me.

He labeled me that way when he first moved into the house next door, back when we played together in a soccer league, back during kindergarten year when I used to call it kinder-*garden*.

Mrs. Garcia—who reminded me so much of my Tía Lupe from El Paso—asked the class to find a partner for another round of "Addition Trivia." Unfortunately, the game didn't go like Mrs. Garcia expected, because everyone in the class simply went after the smartest kids to partner up with.

Needless to say, demand for me wasn't at its highest.

The same couldn't be said of Marco. When it came to anything brain-related, the boy was a total rock star. Half the boys and girls in class circled around him, calling his name.

"Marco, pick me."

"Hey, want to be partners?"

Me . . . I didn't bother. I couldn't think of any reason why he'd want to pair up with someone who scored in the bottom half on most games.

But for some reason, Marco came up and picked me as a partner. Me . . . of all people.

Next thing I knew, I was hearing all sorts of gripes

24

and moans as Marco went on a one-man rampage, answering every question all by himself.

For some reason, I let it get to me and felt the need to prove that I could hold my own in the game. So I chose to raise my hand on the final question.

Marco didn't seem to mind at all. Nope . . . he seemed excited for me. Especially when the question was simple: two plus four.

My heart just about leaped out of my body when I heard Mrs. Garcia ask the question. Anything that required more than two hands was to answer way too hard.

My mind went completely blank, but I wasn't about to take off my shoe and sock to get the answer either.

"Thirteen?" I answered in the form of a question. At least half the kids shook their heads and jeered.

I felt like such a moron. I looked down and pretended not to hear them. It was all I could do to hold back the tears. Mrs. Garcia immediately hushed the class, but there was little she could do about the chuckling.

That's when Marco reached over and literally lifted my head. "Chin up," he said, giving me a smile.

So later that day, when Mrs. Garcia took us out for PE and asked us to pair up for three-legged races across the soccer field, I ignored all the kids now flocking to *me*, hoping my speed would help lead them to victory.

There was only one person I wanted to pair up with. Yep . . . Marco.

That's the day Marco and I became inseparable Best buds.

I don't remember where we placed during the actual race; we just fell over every few feet, laughing the entire time.

Only thing is, I'm not exactly sure about me being a community fish. I'm thinking those kinds of fish are way more responsible and less likely to cause trouble for others. When I'm on the court, playing basketball, I can get a bit aggressive. . . .

And now, seeing the size of some of the fishes—I mean kids—I'm starting to worry how well a community kid like Marco is gonna do in an ocean like this.

"The tall kids are probably just eighth graders," I say, doing my best to make him feel better. "Come on." I wrap my arm around him. "We better find our classes."

Marco and I approach the tables handing out printed student schedules and agendas, which I'm guessing is a fancy word for organizers.

As hopeful as we try to be, we both know we won't

be having any classes together. Marco is GATE identified, as in "Gifted and Talented Education," meaning he'll be placed in all honors classes.

The only honors class *I'm* qualified for is PE—anything involving running—but I'm pretty sure that's not a thing.

Marco follows close behind me and we search for our names. To my surprise, we've got one class together, PE.

I look over at Marco, who's frozen in place, silent. His crinkled forehead and pouting lips tell me everything I need to know.

"Don't worry about it," I say. "I'm sure you'll know plenty of kids from our fifth-grade class. Let's meet up at lunchtime, then go to PE together. Bet you'll make a whole bunch of new friends too."

He gives me a nod, but he looks pretty shaken.

"Dude," I say, "just be yourself. I promise you . . . everyone's gonna love you."

Sure enough, Marco leans in and gives me a hug right there in the open—like it's the last time he's ever going to see me. It's probably not the coolest thing to do—not on the first day of school—but I can't turn him away either.

I make sure to push his head back up.

"Chin up, bro. You got this."

Marco nods, forces a grin, and swallows.

With his schedule in hand, he tugs at his backpack and rolls out in the opposite direction. Seeing him here at school, around so many tall kids, I can't help but notice again how absolutely tiny he really looks.

MARCO

CHAPTER 4

I look back at Isaac, but he's turned around and headed to class. I wish I were as calm about middle school as him. It's strange—this morning I woke up all excited about starting the day. But now, I feel like a tiny sapling in a forest of redwoods.

Mom convinced me there'd be tons of kids my size, but so far, even short kids tower over me. The good news is that the kids don't even notice me, which could also not be so great. I've gotta find a way to change that.

I wonder if the school has a chess club. . . . I could raise a few eyebrows that way for sure.

There's an opening up ahead. The map on the back of my agenda shows it as being the quad area. Whatever it is, there's space to breathe.

I let out a sigh of relief when I spot the familiar faces of Mauricio and Amanda by the drinking fountain.

They wave me over. Suddenly, everything in the world feels okay again. That is until we get close and I notice how much the two of them have grown over the summer—especially Amanda, who wraps her arms around me and awkwardly smooshes my face against her chest.

Amanda scoots back to get a better look at me. "Nice vest. Makes you look all studious."

"I hope so," I say back. "It's kind of the point."

Mauricio shakes my hand, then pulls out his class schedule from his back pocket. "You won't believe this, but Amanda and I have all our classes together, even Office Aide, which I hear is almost never offered to sixth graders."

I lean forward and compare schedules. Not a single class together.

Mauricio takes my schedule and gawks. "Dude, you've got all honors classes!" Both he and Amanda fist-bump and pat me on the shoulder like it's some big deal, when really, I'd rather be in regular, normal classes with my friends.

Suddenly, the bell rings. Mauricio and Amanda say goodbye and head to their class.

I'm left alone, again. This being an odd day on this "alternating" schedule, I've got six minutes to get to my math period, which for some reason doubles as my homeroom . . . just enough time to make a stop at the bathroom.

When I step inside, there's a line of four boys waiting to go. They're pretty tall, probably eighth graders. Fortunately for me, the one low urinal is open. I know it's really meant for students in wheelchairs, but it looks to be just the right size for me.

Since nobody else looks interested in using it, I bypass the line and go pee.

Just as I zip up and turn around, the kid with frosted hair approaches me. He bends down so we are at eye level with each other.

"Oh, how cute." With a giant smirk, he holds up his hand and offers me a high five. "You went all by yourself. You're a big boy now."

What a moron. Like I haven't heard short jokes before. It's kind of sad how proud this guy is of his joke. I raise my hand to high-five him, but he raises his hand up way higher.

I take a deep breath, then jump up to slap my hand against his. Then, as I move past him, I pause and turn to his friends. "You guys do realize that I just peed and haven't washed my hands, right?"

The boys all break out laughing as I leave the room. *Joke's on you, buddy.* Thank goodness for the travel-size bottle of hand sanitizer I keep in my backpack.

Total aggressives, if you ask me.

Now that I think about it, being in honors classes may be better suited for someone like me. More community fish . . . at least, that's what I'm hoping.

First, I've got to find room 308. Fast, before the late bell rings.

I look at the classroom numbers around me: 210, 212. It must be on the third floor.

I push my backpack forward a bit too hard and accidentally bang the back of some kid's shoe. He turns around and glares at me.

"Sorry. My bad," I say, holding both palms up. That's the third flat tire I caused today. I'm starting to wonder if my ZÏPPA might've been a bad idea. Especially going upstairs. Maybe that's why I haven't seen anyone else with rolling backpacks.

I look down at my watch. The bell is going to ring

any minute, but I'm having to go up step by step. I'll definitely have to leave some of my reading books and supplies at home tomorrow.

Yep. There's the bell. I make it to the third floor and hurry to class.

The front door is open. I step closer. On the windowsill beside the door hangs a warning sign: *Mr. Slaughter's Classroom. Enter at Your Own Risk!*

My chest feels like it does whenever my grandma comes to visit, and she squeezes all the air out of me with one of her famous bear hugs. I can feel my anxiety start to build. No, not now. The last thing I need is one of my episodes.

I rub the back of my neck and take a few long breaths.

"Please . . . come on in," calls out a low, bassy voice.

My hands start to quiver. I picture a monster of a man waiting at the door. The teacher might as well be calling out, *Fee-fi-fo-fum.* I look down at the floor and take a moment to gather myself. Get a grip, *Marco*.

Suddenly, a pair of giant-sized loafers stop in front of me. "Welcome to my class. I'm Mr. Slaughter." I pan upward until I'm . . . almost eye to eye with him?

Mr. Slaughter looks on with a bearded smile and a Santa Claus twinkle in his eyes. Mr. Slaughter is just a little taller than me. Four or five inches at the most!

"Hey, buddy," he says. "Please, join us."

My legs immediately unfreeze, and I take the last available seat right up front.

"Okay, scholars," he says, walking along the middle aisle. "Let's go ahead and get started. My name is Mr. Slaughter. I am your sixth-grade math teacher for the year."

A moppy-haired boy at the back of the room mumbles something. I turn and notice a few other students giving him a look.

Mr. Slaughter's right brow rises. "Well, that certainly didn't take long." He circles the room and stops inches from the boy. "Just so you know, I've got great hearing. So, to answer your question, no . . . I am not a sixth grader too."

The boy sinks down in his seat, red as a tomato.

Good. Serves him right. Poor Mr. Slaughter. I know all about short jokes.

Mr. Slaughter walks back to the front of the room, still smiling. "Look, guys. I'm short. I get it." Again, he scans the room—only now the twinkle in his eyes is missing. "How about we get all the short jokes out of the way?"

The room stays silent.

"Here," Mr. Slaughter says, "I'll go first. You guys want to know why I no longer teach eighth grade?" This time, he looks in my direction as he pauses. "I simply got tired of my students *looking down* on me." He winks at the class and slaps the side of his knee.

A few of the kids chuckle.

"Yeah, and in case you are wondering, no, I have never won teacher of the year. Guess I keep getting *overlooked.*" His second joke gets a few more laughs.

"Oh, and for those of you wondering, yes, I am also the school's cross-country coach. We'll be running mostly on the school's grass field this year . . . and yes, the blades of grass do tickle my armpits as I run."

The twinkle in Mr. Slaughter's eyes is back, and he's got the whole class dying of laughter.

"The school year will be a lot of work, but it will be lots of fun. Of course, you guys will have to explain all your jokes to me, because they tend to go . . . *over my head.*"

I'm laughing so hard that the sides of my stomach hurt.

He continues. "I'm so glad to be a teacher. Just wish the pay were better. Sometimes, I struggle to put food on the table. You know, because it's too high."

Mr. Slaughter's eyes close as he laughs along with us.

"All right, scholars. Now that we got the jokes out of the way, why don't we begin by introducing ourselves to our neighbors."

I turn around to a group of boys. Oscar, Jorge, and Orlando already seem to know each other.

I lean in, offering a fist bump like Isaac taught me to do. Only each of the kids shakes my fist instead. Must be something middle school kids are doing. I make a mental note for later.

Turns out the boys all know each other from their previous school and start talking about my favorite anime, My Hero Academia, and ask if I follow it.

I shake my head excitedly.

The guys are super nice. Definitely community fish.

I think I'm going to love middle school.

ISAAC

CHAPTER 5

After a bit of roaming, I eventually get to the 200 Building and find my homeroom with a . . . Ms. Patricia Kempe, who is also my language arts teacher. I walk up to the closed door and peek inside. There's a tall woman standing by the corner of the room, wearing wireless earbuds and drinking coffee out of a rainbow mug. I look closely and spot a blue stud on the side of her nose.

"Do you know Ms. Kempe? I hear she's awesome," a voice calls out from behind me.

I turn and spot a kid with a tight buzz cut smiling at me.

"Both my older sister and brother had her," he says. "They say she's one of the best teachers at this school.

And get this"—he looks around as if he's telling me a secret—"she doesn't believe in giving out homework."

My eyes bug out. "No homework? I like her already." I hold out a fist. "I'm Isaac."

"Yeah, I know." The boy fist-bumps and smiles. "Alexxander, with two *x*'s. But my friends call me Dos Equis, you know . . . like the beer."

Dos Equis? Sadly, I know all about it. It's one of Apá's go-to beers.

There's something oddly familiar about him, and I can't help but wonder where I've seen him before.

"Dude, you've got a killer first step."

"You've seen me play?" I ask.

"Yep. This summer . . . on the All-Baller Travel League. We faced off for the championship."

"Wait, you play point guard, right?"

"Yep. Would have led the league in assists"—he opens his eyes wide and playfully gives me a funny look—"if it wasn't for *somebody* who shut me down on that final game."

"Aw, man, you are good. You caused me all sorts of trouble." I lean in and bro-hug my fellow baller. "Man, you've got mad handles. I love your behind-the-back crossover."

38

"Thanks, but it looks like we get to be teammates from here on. I hear Coach Chavez is really good."

WhenI think about Luis, Nick, Ryan, Saul, me, *and* him all on the same team, I just about salivate. "This year's team's gonna destroy."

"No doubt. It's gonna be *back*-to-*back*-to-*back* championships." Again, he fist-bumps me. "Nice Lakers jersey, by the way. Big fan?"

"I sweat purple and gold. How about you?"

He points to his Lakers socks and Lakers belt buckle, before raising his shirt up to reveal his Lakers underwear waistband. "What do *you* think?"

"Pretty cool." I start digging into my backpack, searching for my Lakers pencil case full of ticket stubs I've collected with Apá, when Alexxander—I mean Dos Equis—taps me on the shoulder. "She's coming."

The second Ms. Kempe opens the door, the kids waiting beside us pour into the room. Dos Equis tosses his backpack onto the seat next to him and waves me over.

I can't help but smile too. Five minutes into middle school and I've made my first new friend. Hope Marco's having the same luck.

Right away, Ms. Kempe addresses the class. Dos Equis is right. She seems really nice *and* funny. She starts class by telling us all about her first day of middle school and how she failed to fit in anywhere. She even shared how half the teachers assumed she was a troublemaker based on the way she dressed.

Somewhere between jokes, she also goes over her classroom expectations and grading policy. Then, just as class is about to end, she casually adds one more piece. "Oh yeah . . . and no homework here."

The class erupts in cheers.

Second-period science class isn't as much fun. Mr. Widén goes over his class syllabus, only he never cracks a single joke, except when he introduces Skellington Boneapart III, his model skeleton. Poor Skellie has two front teeth missing and a dislocated lower jaw that someone reattached using paper clips. Fifteen minutes into class and kids are already joking that Skellington's possibly a former student of Mr. Widén, one who died of boredom during one of his lectures.

I'm just glad he's nice.

Since Marco and I both have the same lunch, we can meet up in no time. When the bell rings, I hurry down the stairs. The lunch area is already packed tight with kids. I search the lunch line for him. Nothing.

However, I do spot a few friends from fifth grade.

40

Luis, Nick, Ryan, and Saul are in line together. Their NBA jerseys make them easy to spot. I haven't seen them since our summer league.

Man, I can't wait to meet up with them again—but not without Marco. Even though he doesn't play ball, I'm sure he's gonna love hanging with the guys as much as I do.

The cafeteria is as huge as it is noisy. I scan the rows of tables but don't have much luck finding him.

That's when I hear my name. Sure enough, Marco's standing on the table bench, waving like he's signaling an approaching airplane.

I wrap my arm around my backpack and rush over.

"Everyone," Marco announces, "this is my best friend, Isaac."

I head-nod to everyone. "'Sup, guys?"

Only they don't do that back. Oscar, Jorge, and a boy they call Orlando each take turns standing and introducing themselves.

"Pleased to meet you."

"Pleasure is mine."

Leave it to Marco to find the most well-mannered kids in the universe. A tableful of Marcos. As much as I'd rather join up with my buddies, I also don't want to be the rude one of the bunch. I take a seat next to Marco.

The group shares their food by pooling their lunches and forming a buffet table. I reach for my Tupperware container with the fresh fruit salad Amá made for me and add it to the collection. Then I pull out my ham and cheese torta as I extend my feet beside Marco's ZÏPPA. That's when I glance over at the table beside us. Dos Equis is sitting with what look to be eighth-grade boys. He sees me and nods. I nod back at him before switching my attention to Orlando, who randomly asks which coding language I like best. A question better suited for Marco.

"Coding language?" I say, stalling for time.

"Yeah, you know, like Java, C++, Python?"

The entire table freezes and waits for my answer. I think back to the summer when Marco tried teaching me to program a video game. "Personally, I like Scratch," I say, purposely leaving out the fact that it's the only coding form I know anything about.

"Scratch? That's just grab and drop," says Orlando. "Isn't that a bit elementary?"

The whole bunch of them turn to each other uncomfortably, as if someone at the table has just farted.

Suddenly, I'm feeling pretty stupid—like this table might be a bit too smart for someone like me.

"I love using Scratch too," Marco chimes in just in time. "It's totally retro. I've got a whole collection of games I've made."

Orlando agrees. "We should share all our games with each other . . . maybe check each other's code."

Okay, forget the whole feeling stupid part; I'm now feeling like a complete moron. My mind races and I get an idea. "Yeah, that sounds great, but I'm gonna line up for a snack."

Marco's brow creases. "Why? You haven't even touched your torta."

"I know," I say. "I'm just not in the mood for it."

Orlando jumps at the opportunity. "Can I have your torta?"

My stomach practically calls out to it. Ham, cheese, and refried beans—my favorite. As hungry as I am, I'm more desperate to get away from the table.

"Sure," I say. With that, I head over to the lunch line and take my place at the back. Fortunately for me, the line is long enough that I spend the rest of my break waiting.

Hmm . . . wonder if I can convince Marco to give *my* friends a try.

MARCO

CHAPTER 6

What a day! So far, school has been better than I could have imagined. The kids in my classes are super friendly and smart too. I've already made all sorts of friends, like Oscar, Jorge, and Orlando. The three of them invited me to join both the Robotics and Coding clubs after school with them, which sound amazing. Only . . . I think I'm going to pass. I promised myself I'd do a sport this year. And middle school offers so many options, there has to be one I'm good at.

I can't wait to tell Isaac all about Mr. Slaughter. He's not going to believe me. Fortunately, we both have PE together, which is where I'm heading. So far, there's no sign of Isaac. I lost track of him after he went to buy a snack at lunch.

With lunch hour now over, I follow a wave of kids into the boys' locker room. It's super loud and wild. A real zoo. Kids of all sizes crowd the place, slamming the metal lockers and hollering.

The noise rattles me. So does the smell. I take a minute to breathe, but I can't ignore the cringy language echoing around me, words I'm not supposed to hear. I'm definitely not in elementary school anymore.

I check my agenda for my locker number: 113. Some people might be worried by the number. Not me. In many countries, thirteen is thought to be lucky and powerful.

With my locker and combination in hand, I head to the first aisle, where a bunch of half-dressed boys holler at their friends across the room. I'm talking major aggressives. The idea of having to strip down to my underwear in front of them creeps me out a bit. Some of them look like they should be in high school. While classes might be separated by grade level, it doesn't seem to be the case with the locker room.

I find my locker and take a seat on the bench. To each side of me are two kids who look old enough to shave. The loud one with the frosted hair is that same kid who tried making fun of me earlier in the restroom.

I try not to hyperventilate.

Thank goodness he's too distracted by slapping his friend with his rolled-up shirt to notice me. It's probably just an excuse to show off his crazy six-pack. I look down at the name Sharpied onto his shorts in bold, sloppy letters: *Byron Miller.*

I turn myself around and hurry to get my backpack into the locker. Only it doesn't fit. You'd think the school would provide bigger lockers, like the ones on TV. But I can't worry about that now. I've got to get dressed before Byron Miller or his friend notice me.

I slip my shirt off over my head and can't help but notice how lumpy, almost Jell-O-ish my body is.

Seriously, I look nothing like those two boys.

For some reason, I have no muscle tone. Like . . . none at all! It's like someone removed all the muscles from inside my body.

Right then, Byron Miller lets out a huge cackle as he stares and points at me. Luckily, that's the moment one of the coaches arrives. "Attention, everybody!" calls out the teacher over a megaphone.

Everyone around me freezes.

"My name is Mr. Chavez. I run this place." He adjusts the waistband of his low-fitting shorts, which seems to hold up his belly. "Most of you should have figured out which lockers belong to you. And since everyone but one of you"—he gives a dirty look to a kid standing beside him—"came in for orientation and picked up your uniforms, we're gonna have you guys change out. From there, you will be assigned numbers for attendance purposes."

He sighs. "I also want to remind the eighth graders to be welcoming to our newbies." He turns straight in the direction of the boy with the frosted hair. "This means no locker slamming, no screaming, no pantsing, no wrist burns, no body blows, no purple nurples, no wet willies, or any other stupid thing you kids can come up with. Is that clear?"

The boy nods, but the smirk he gives his friend as the teacher looks away definitely says otherwise.

ISAAC

CHAPTER 7

After waiting around in the lunch line for twenty minutes, I eventually end up with a half-frozen slice of cheese pizza, a bruised apple, and chunky chocolate milk I refuse to drink. Immediately, I fling the entire lunch into the trash. I'm still hungry but settle for a red sports drink from the vending machine. The drink is ice cold—just the way I like it—but it can't replace the ham, cheese, and refried bean torta I left behind.

When the lunch bell rings, I rush over to meet up with Marco, only he and his friends are long gone. It's no big deal. I'll see him next period in PE.

I go inside the boys' locker room. It's hard to believe that the place could smell so bad after only half a day of classes. Then again, Amá says I'm already starting to smell like day-old cheeseburger, even with just a few straggly hairs on my pits.

I pass a group of boys kicking a dead roach around like it's a soccer ball. There's no sign of Marco. I do, however, find my locker in the bottom row. I reach for my lock. But as I spin the combination pad to the left, my mind has a major brain fart.

What was my padlock combination? 12-26-32? 12-32-22? I search my pockets for my little sticker with the numbers on it.

I remember slipping the tiny sticker into my pants pocket . . . *last night!*

I can picture my cargo pants crumpled up into a ball on the floor—next to my bed—not folded neatly in my hamper like Amá asked me to do . . . *over and over again.*

My inner voice tells me not to freak out, that Amá doesn't expect me to be perfect or anything even close to that. That my best is all she wants. But then there's this other voice, the one I call Enrique (don't ask), telling me to punch my hand through the locker. Don't worry, I know better than to listen to him.

Anyway, I'm trying a few more combinations when Dos Equis takes a seat two lockers down. Apparently, he and I share PE.

"Hey, Dos Equis," I say as casually as I can in an effort to sound as cool as him.

He looks over at me and nods. Then, with super swag, he slides down the bench. "Hey, bro, you should hang with my table at lunch."

My Enrique voice is yippee-ing at the top of its lungs. I mean, making friends with those eighth graders would be way awesome.

My ears perk up, and I can't help but smile.

Dos Equis scoots in even closer. "Hey, you don't have to hang out with those dorks."

Wait. What? I do my best not to get mad. I mean, he doesn't know Marco like I do. I'm pretty sure Dos Equis would change his tune if he got to know him.

"Thanks," I say, forcing a smile. "I'll let you know." *Yeah, right.*

Dos Equis shrugs. "All right, man. But just so you know, this *is* middle school. Reps matter. My older brother taught me that around here you're only as cool as your friends."

I'm flattered that he thinks I'm cool enough to hang with him at his table, but then again, I'm annoyed that he's just called Marco a dork.

"You sure?" he asks again, as if surprised anyone

would pass up an offer from him.

"Nuh. Like I said, I'm good."

"All right, bro. Whatever." He brushes me off, annoyed.

My Enrique voice is pretty upset too.

I toss my stuff into my locker and shut the door. Without the combo, there is no way of locking up my stuff, but there's nothing in there worth stealing. My biggest concern is finding Marco and making sure *he's* okay. Making sure he hasn't come across any other kids like Dos Equis.

Next aisle over, I spot Luis, Nick, Ryan, and Saul waving over to me. I wave back. On the court—even against kids one to two years older than us—the five of us are unstoppable, which is huge since there is only a varsity team this year, due to budget cuts.

Suddenly, our PE teacher enters the room and warns us about doing stupid things that I've only heard about on online memes. When he's done, I peek around at the first row. Sure enough, there's Marco . . . sitting on the bench between two eighth graders in his underwear, calm as can be.

That's the part of Marco I envy most—his confidence. The way he's hella sure of himself, you'd think he'd have amazing abs or toned arms of his own.

He's also got this gift for making friends, and I don't really want to get in the way of that. So I step out of the locker room and wait for him outside by our numbers like Mr. Chavez instructed.

The asphalt is hot to the touch, enough that it burns our butts. But Mr. Chavez insists that everyone take a seat—in numeric order. He butchers our names as he calls them out.

Ryan and Nick from my summer league sit on either side of me at numbers seven and nine. Talk about good luck.

We fist-bump and—after a bad why-is-six-afraid-of-seven joke—we go over our entire schedules. Turns out we've got two more classes together later in the day.

Wish I could say the same for me and Marco.

Marco, by the way, sits way toward the back on number twenty-seven. I look over and wave. He jazz-hands me back like he hasn't seen me in days.

Mr. Chavez has us do some stretching exercises before running laps. Of course, the second he puts down his megaphone, I take Nick and Ryan over to see Marco, who was easily our loudest fan this summer at our games.

Marco's adjusting the waistband of his PE shorts, which are hiked up so high, it's like he's wearing suspenders. Neither Nick nor Ryan seems to notice, or care. "Guys, you remember Marco?"

"Heck yeah . . . how could we forget our one-man cheering squad?" says Nick.

Both boys nod and offer up a fist bump.

Marco wraps his hands around their fists and shakes them—something I've never seen him do before. "The two of you are amazing on the court."

I'm about to bury my head in shame. Thankfully, they think it's funny and laugh it off.

That's when a whistle sounds off and everyone—except for two boys busy trying to pants each other—turns in attention. Mr. Chavez's eyebrows drop, and he turns toward the boys, blowing his whistle so hard that his face turns bright red and his khaki shorts drop down well below his gut.

This time both boys stop and stand in fear. Only Mr. Chavez is too winded to say a word. He raises his hand and points to the grass field. "Three . . . laps . . . everyone!" he finally calls out.

All at once, everyone bursts onto the field, an actual stampede of kids.

I turn to Marco, who is by the side, biting his lower lip, waiting for an opening to join in. He's looking about as unsure as a kid trying to enter a fast-paced game of double Dutch jump rope.

"Come on, Marco," I call out. "Just start running."

He hikes up his shorts again and begins to run—well, kind of. I race over beside him, urging him to speed it up.

Marco tightens his fists and crinkles his forehead and I look on, bracing myself for his burst of speed. Only . . . it doesn't come.

In fact, just his hands begin to pump faster. I think back to our elementary years and try to remember if I've ever seen him run. But come to think of it, the answer is a big fat no. During fifth-grade PE, Ms. Hanson had him helping her out, serving as scorer and timekeeper on account of how good he is with numbers.

I look around. The only kids going at this pace are the ones walking behind us at the very end—and even they seem to be gaining ground.

I slow down to a crawl and stay at his side. "You got this, bro! Now how 'bout some longer strides?"

Marco flashes me a quick smile, locks focus with the ground in front of him, and goes into some sort of skip-step that reminds me of Winnie-the-Pooh's bouncing Tigger. Only, it's not any faster.

Like hummingbird wings, his arms pump up and down in a frenzy. Now if only they'd somehow sync up with his legs.

Two more groups of kids pass us by. Marco turns and waves them by. Now we're officially at the back, but Marco continues his own unique pace.

I feel like plopping him over my shoulder and catching up to the last group. Seriously, how does this not bother him?

"Hey," a snarky, scratchy voice calls out. It's from one of the two eighth-grade boys. One of them is that same tower-of-a-kid who bumped me earlier, the one with the highlights. "Where's that rolling cooler of yours?" he adds.

What a cheap shot. I glance over at Marco, who smiles back at him anyway. "It's not a cooler, Byron. It's a ZÏPPA."

"Yeah, the wheels are really smooth," I chime in, trying to help.

The two eighth-grade boys exchange a look, then break into obnoxious laughter.

"Ignore him," says Marco. "That's just Byron and

his friend. They're total aggressives."

That's when Byron turns back and opens his big mouth. "That's good," he says, "means you can use it like a stroller to wheel your little friend around." And just like that, the two accelerate past us.

Marco's arms stop pumping, and his head slumps down—and so do his shoulders. He looks shaken. He looks . . . hurt.

My blood boils. "Don't worry about it, Marco. Those guys are just trying to act all cool." That's when I make up my mind. "Let's see how cool they feel after they get beat by a sixth grader."

I take a deep breath and chase behind them before Marco can try talking me out of it. My sights are locked ahead on the two boys. Besides being taller and older, they also have stalky, almost ostrichlike legs. It practically takes me two steps to match each of theirs. But it doesn't matter—all those years of playing basketball have made me pretty fast.

Right away, I pass one group of kids, then another. I'm really close but wait for a turn to make my move.

I swing my elbow around Byron and cut in front of him. "Oh, my bad . . . I didn't realize this was the slow lane."

The two boys accelerate right behind me. I can practically feel their huffing and puffing along the back of my neck. This was a bad idea. These kids are legit fast, and I'm not sure I can keep this up.

I've got to figure out why I always get myself into situations like this! Gotta learn to think things through better. And not getting enough sleep last night isn't helping either.

As I'm thinking, a sharp pain hits my side. Only, it's definitely not a cramp—just Byron, who purposely elbowed me while passing.

I grab my side and watch him and his friend move up ahead.

No way I'm gonna let this go. Pain or no pain, I've got to teach them a lesson. Unlike those two, I do know a thing or two about keeping pace. I stay back, but never enough that they get away from me. We circle the field—and are about to lap Marco—when Byron's friend gives up. Now the race is between Byron and me.

I glance over at Marco. He's no longer running. Neither are the kids gathering around him. I recognize a few faces from elementary school. Their arms are up in the air, and they are fist-pumping and cheering—for me, I think! Guess they don't like Byron either.

All of a sudden, I feel a surge of energy rushing through me.

"Okay, buddy," I say to myself. "This is for you."

I quicken my pace and catch Byron looking over his shoulder. The smart thing would be to stay close and wait for the right moment to pass him. But after what he said to Marco—after the elbow he planted on me—I don't want to just beat him. I want to embarrass him.

The two of us are now in a total sprint. This time, there's a horrible knot starting to form at the center of my gut, but there's a crowd gathered by the finish line, and I'm not about to give up now.

We cut the final turn neck to neck. From the sound of Byron's breathing, he's just as tired as I am. But. I. Refuse. To. Lose.

I take a big gulp of air and push myself to run faster than I've ever run before. The finish line is up ahead. I lean forward, my chest and neck extended as far as possible.

My stomach rumbles as I approach the final steps. I turn my head and peek over at Byron, who is a good half foot behind me.

I take the final plunge forward and beat him with enough space to make me the clear winner. Kids I don't even know are running up to me, offering high fives all around. Even Mr. Chavez hurries over and takes a spot beside Byron, who is keeled over, gasping for air.

Mr. Chavez looks down at my name Sharpied onto my shorts. "Isaac Castillo?"

He jots a note on his clipboard. "Not bad. Not bad at all. Of course, that would've been much more impressive . . . had you done all three of your laps."

Wait—what?

Byron seems to suddenly revive. "Hear that, everyone? He cheated. Castillo here is a cheater!"

I look around at the kids who just congratulated me a second ago. The smiles and cheers now become frowns and jeers. A few literally boo me.

My gut tightens and churns. And before I can say a word, I'm spewing vomit like one of those geysers at Yellowstone National Park.

Mr. Chavez is glaring at me.

I wipe my mouth on my shirtsleeve and stare down at his sneakers. I can't believe what I've just done.

Almost doglike, Mr. Chavez lifts a leg and tries his best to shake off the chunky red pieces sticking to his shoes, socks, and leg hairs. "Man . . . not my brand-new Hokas!"

MARCO

CHAPTER 8

Mr. Chavez isn't happy about his shoes and has us all run extra laps while he hoses himself down by the grass field.

I feel bad about what happened. Feel like it's my fault that Isaac made himself sick. I offered to take him to the nurse's office, but Mr. Chavez wasn't having it. He said that of everyone there, I needed the most practice.

Guess he's right about that. I mean, it's not like I don't try. I swear I do. I pump my hands and do my best to copy the movement of the other kids, only I seem to move in slow motion like in a bad dream. It's like neither of my legs knows which leg is supposed to take the lead first.

Of course, most of the other kids finish before I do

and have already gone into the locker room to change. Only now, Mr. Chavez is gone. He's probably inside, changing his shoes.

I'm the last to head over to the water fountain on the side of the building. When I push the button, I feel my feet leave the ground. I turn to look behind me. It's Byron Miller, picking me up.

"Here you go, minion. Now you can reach the faucet."

I squirm and kick my feet, but he's holding on to me real tight.

"Dude, what are you doing? Put me down."

"Put you down? Nope, not just yet."

The boy carries me over by the locker room entrance, where a buddy of his wraps his sweatshirt around me like it's one of those baby carriers parents use.

"Come on. This isn't funny," I say, practically begging. But the boy acts like he doesn't even hear me. Then, as if this wasn't humiliating enough, he parades me in front of a group of kids, two of which I recognize back from elementary school. But instead of helping me, they scramble backward as if they didn't see a thing.

Highlights boy laughs and shifts me into his arms, cradling me like I'm a baby.

I'm so angry that a tear escapes down the side of my face.

I then feel a tug at the back of my shorts. Byron Miller pulls them down enough that everyone around sees the back side of my underwear. "Maybe we should check if he had an accident?"

That's when a voice stops him. "Hey, knock it off!"

Thank God. I turn to look. It's Nick and Ryan. Friends of Isaac. Great players. Isaac calls them part of their dream team. I now see why. They're a real dream come true!

Byron finally puts me down and turns his attention to the two of them. "Really. You two gonna make me?"

Nick smirks and flashes his phone. "I recorded everything you did."

Byron goes pale. I make a break for it and rush next to Nick, who rests his arm on my shoulder.

"You mess with him again, and I show the video to the principal."

Highlights grinds his teeth but doesn't move or say a word.

Finally, the bell rings. "Come on, Marco," says Ryan. "We gotcha, homie."

With that we go inside the locker room to change.

ISAAC
CHAPTER 9

Next thing I know, I'm waiting at the nurse's office, sandwiched on a couch between a kid holding a cold pack over his bloody nose and a kid with a staple wedged deep into his thumb.

The door finally opens. A boy with bandaged knees in PE shorts limps in stiffly.

The nurse turns and glances over at us through thick glasses. "Isaac?"

Somehow, the lady looks familiar, looks like . . . "Ms. Ornelas?"

"¡Ay!" she says. "I can't believe it's you." She reaches out for a hug but pulls back the second she catches a whiff of the puke smell on me.

Ms. Ornelas used to be the nurse at my elementary

school. A super-nice lady. She took care of me when I broke my leg jumping off the swings, in first *and* third grade.

"Sorry," I say, "I barely recognized you with your new short hair."

She runs her fingers through her hair and sways her head side to side like she's inside some shampoo commercial. "Yeah, I couldn't stand having long hair another day. Not with all this heat we've been having." She looks me over from head to toe. "You smell like you had a bad lunch."

"Yeah, I threw up all over Mr. Chavez's shoes."

The boy with the ice pack sets it down and grins wide enough to show his missing back teeth. "No way. Really?"

"Wish I could've seen that." Staple Boy offers me a high five, but I point to his injured thumb. He nods and offers me his other hand.

"Do you feel okay?" Ms. Ornelas asks me. "Any diarrhea?"

Really? She asks in front of everyone! Thank God it's not that. I'd rather have a staple in my finger than to ever have to admit that openly.

I shake my head. "No. I think I just pushed myself too hard."

She presses her lips together. "I'm sure you're right. But we have a firm one-barf rule at this school. Wait here. I'll try reaching your parents. Have one of them come pick you up. Okay?"

"Seriously, I feel fine. There's no need to call home. Besides, my Amá's at work, managing her restaurant, so I doubt she'll even hear her phone."

"What about your dad? He's a contractor. *He* shouldn't have a problem stepping away for a bit, right?"

"Yeah, I guess," I say back.

She's right. Apá doesn't do much of the physical labor anymore. Pretty much just tells his guys what to do. He should be able to come get me without a problem.

Ms. Ornelas pulls up my records on her computer. "I'll try your dad's cell number."

I take a seat, wondering if Apá's new address will pop up too. Dad answers right away. I can't hear what he says, but whatever it is, it makes Ms. Ornelas laugh out loud.

She says something back, but she speaks so quickly

that her Spanish is tough to understand, at least for me.

After a bit, she hangs up, smiling. "Sit tight. He'll be here shortly." I lean back in my chair, watching Ms. Ornelas make her rounds. First, she strolls over to Bloody-Nose Boy, gently pulling his forehead forward. "Mijo, you got to keep your head down, okay? Otherwise, you simply swallow the blood." She then takes a close look at the staple in the other boy's finger and rolls her eyes. "¡Pero qué muchachos! You're the second kid today."

The boy looks down at the floor in shame.

"Come on. I have a staple remover in my desk," she says with a wink.

At first, waiting around for Apá to pick me up is kind of cool. I get to see all the stupid things kids do. If stapling your own finger isn't bad enough, another kid wearing a Pokémon backpack comes in with a pencil eraser stuck inside his ear. He keeps swearing that he doesn't know how it got in there, even with the eraserless pencil sticking out of his backpack pocket.

Ms. Ornelas keeps her cool, though—even tells him he isn't the first kid to stick an eraser in his ear. About fifteen minutes later, an older girl, probably an eighth grader, comes in claiming to have really bad cramps—guess she must've been running hard too. She's handed a warming pad and told to lie down for a bit.

That's when I catch Ms. Ornelas looking over at the clock. It's been thirty-five minutes since she called. Apá is never late. . . . Well, that was before he moved out a few weeks ago. For whatever reason, the move seems to have affected his memory. Family game nights. League basketball games. Dentist appointments. He's forgotten them all.

But I don't get all mad about it like Amá.

I'm mostly used to it by now. Having Apá forget is kind of like getting a paper cut on your finger. Sure, the initial sting bothers you at first, but for the most part, you slap on a Band-Aid and forget about it.

Unless of course someone like Ms. Ornelas keeps asking questions about why Apá is running late, and I have to come up with excuses for him again.

"I'm sure it's probably just the traffic," I say. "The condo my dad is remodeling is on the other side of town." Only I can't seem to look up when I say it. It's like the guilt weighs down my head.

Having to come up with excuses for him feels like lemon juice seeping deep into my Band-Aid, which can hurt a lot more than the cut itself—like the time Amá couldn't meet with one of my teachers last year because my abuelito was sick.

She asked Apá to meet with my fifth-grade teacher, Ms. Hanson, about my missing too many assignments. Only he never showed. Ms. Hanson and I sat in the principal's meeting room, waiting.

I told Ms. Hanson about how sometimes his boss calls him out to the middle of nowhere and expects him to run emergency jobs, but I could tell by the way she looked at me that she wasn't buying any of it.

And here is Ms. Ornelas, looking at me in the exact same way. "No, mijo," she says, refilling her jar of sugar-free lollipops. "He told me he was at home, enjoying his day off."

His day off? My stomach starts to churn.

Part of the reason my parents separated was because Amá didn't want me seeing Apá drunk again. I overheard her telling him that he needed to sober up if he wanted to be part of my life.

At first, Apá argued that he had things under control and that she was being ridiculous. Then Amá mentioned the idea of me growing up to be like him.

Apá didn't say anything back, so I peeked outside my

68

room and caught him coming out of the garage with a suitcase in hand.

I shut the door and listened as he returned to the master bedroom, only no one spoke another word. All I could hear was him packing up his things.

I rushed outside as I heard the front door open and close. Apá's eyes were glassy and pink, only this time, drinking had nothing to do with it.

He put his suitcase down, reached over toward me, and held me really tight. "Mijo," he said, "I'll be better . . . promise."

It was the same promise I'd made Amá.

I look over at the clock, knowing all too well how tough it is to keep a promise like that.

Come on, Apá.

His downtown apartment is only like ten minutes away. I try to stay calm and not rush to any conclusions. For all I know, Apá really could be stuck in traffic or outside, circling the parking lot in search of a parking spot.

I reach for Ms. Ornelas's metal trash can and bring it closer to me. Suddenly, I'm feeling sick again.

MARCO

CHAPTER 10

Nick and Ryan invite me over to change by their locker, where it's safer, but I'm worried about getting in trouble with Mr. Chavez. Then again, even that is better than going back to my locker alone.

I slip off my shirt. My entire body is trembling, only it has nothing to do with the temperature of the room.

Nick comes over and pats me on the shoulder. "Don't worry about him."

"Yeah," chimes in Ryan. "That's just Byron. Nick and I once played in a basketball league with him. He's a real jerk. Thinks he can get away with anything just because of how good he is on the court. He loves picking on kids smaller than him."

"But *everyone* is smaller than him," I say, pushing

my head through my undershirt.

Nick laughs hard. Ryan laughs even harder.

"Nick, Ryan"—I struggle to find the right words— "I'm really glad you guys helped me out and all . . . but I'm not sure I like the idea of anyone seeing that video, even the principal. He'll probably have to show it to my mom. And I really—"

"No worries," says Nick. "There's no video. I made it up. The big dummy fell for it."

I look down at my hands and feet; the trembling has stopped. That's when Mr. Chavez enters the room with his soggy sneakers sloshing under him. "Listen up, everyone! A quick reminder that we will be having try-outs for our basketball team next week. And yes, you heard me right. This year, the school only has enough funds for only one team."

He looks over at Nick and Ryan. "I expect to see the two of you there. Your summer league coach sent me highlights of your championship game. It was a bit blurry, but even so, I liked what I saw." He points over at Ryan. "Especially you, Mr. Twenty-Five. Not too many players can completely shut down an entire team like you did."

Ryan shakes his head. "Thanks, but I'm not number

twenty-five. That's Isaac. The boy who threw up on y—"

Nick smacks him on the arm.

Mr. Chavez looks down at his wet shoes. "Really. *That* kid?"

"Yes, sir. Me and Nick both play wing. Isaac's really a shooting guard, but being the best passer, he played point guard for us."

"Yeah," adds Nick. "Isaac can pretty much score whenever he wants, but he's a real team player—even led the league in assists."

"I'll be darned." Mr. Chavez rubs his chin. "We've got a kid coming in—his name is Alexxander, with two *x*'s. Goes by 'Dos Equis.' Anyway, kid's a true point. He's got more handles than"—he looks down at his belly—"well, me."

We all laugh, but only after he does first.

"All right. Tell your friend that I'll see him on the court . . . if he can keep his lunch down." With that, Mr. Chavez disappears into his office, leaving a trail of wet shoeprints behind him.

"With Isaac on your team, you guys should be unstoppable," I say. "This one time, I watched him out-score the entire opposing team, *all by himself.* His dad took us both to dinner to celebrate."

Both boys nod like they've seen it happen too.

"Hey," Ryan suddenly blurts out, "you should try out with us."

"Yeah," says Nick. "You and Isaac are best friends, so you must play too, right?"

Play? I think back to the last few times Isaac and I played on his driveway. I just kind of stood there with my hands up while he shot from all over the court, which was fine with me, because anytime I tried dribbling the ball, I ended up tripping over it or jamming my finger on the ball.

The only time I didn't get hurt was when I helped Isaac measure and spray-paint the court lines on his driveway. "'Play' probably isn't the right word."

Nick pats my back. "Man, sounds like this homie don't mess around on the court." He turns to me. "Can you hang with Isaac?"

Hang? That's a strange question to ask. Isaac and I are best friends. We've hung out together since kindergarten. "Of course I can hang with him. In fact, he's been trying to shake me for years. Hasn't happened yet," I say jokingly.

73

The guys share a look like they can't believe what I'm saying.

"You must be all savage on the court, huh?" asks Nick. Only he doesn't wait for an answer. "We could really use someone like you."

Like me?

"I'm not sure—"

"Dude," Ryan cuts me off mid-sentence. "You can be the Muggsy Bogues of our team."

"Muggsy Bogues?"

"He was the smallest player in NBA history but a real legend. All five feet three inches of him. He was a beast. All the players were super scared of dribbling around him."

Five foot three? Suddenly, all sorts of images run through my mind. Which is kind of dumb because I've never played the game before—not really. Visions of me running down the court in a real uniform holding a championship trophy, visions of me getting a steal and running down for an easy layup. Visions of my dad in the stands . . . cheering for me—a real dream come true.

"So, are you trying out?" Ryan asks.

Try out? Me?

74

Me playing ball is ridiculous, really . . . but the idea that someone five feet three inches tall actually made the NBA has me thinking.

I suppose it's doable, right? There's a week until tryouts. And it's just middle school. I could go home, watch a few tutorials, even practice with Isaac. I mean, if you really think about it, it's just throwing a ball into a hoop. How hard can that possibly be?

"Yeah," I finally say. "I think I *will* try out."

With that said, both boys walk me all the way back to the 200 Building, where my next class is.

"You guys didn't need to walk me over," I tell them.

"Just want to make sure no one messes with our teammate."

I blush.

"Well, thanks for your help out there."

"No sweat," says Nick while holding out his fist to me. I'm about to fist-bump him back when I remember Oscar, Jorge, and Orlando cupping my hand earlier. As strange as it is, I'm guessing this is now a thing, something middle schoolers do.

Again, for the second time today, I reach out and shake his fist.

He laughs. "Mugs, dude . . . you're funny."

Mugs?

Wait, did I just get my very first nickname? A real nickname. A jock nickname! Oh my God, wait till Isaac hears about this.

ISAAC

CHAPTER 11

It's now been a whole hour. I never realized how busy the nurse's office can get. Most of the kids are coming in with stomachaches. It's really making me start to question the cafeteria food. Three out of four times, Ms. Ornelas simply asks if they need to visit the bathroom. And guess who gets to sit here, a few feet from the door. The sounds are so bad, I'm actually considering sticking an eraser into each of my own ears.

Another thirty minutes pass. That's when a curly-haired kid with a set of scraped knees limps in all zombielike. His PE uniform and face are covered in orange dirt from the baseball field.

Ms. Ornelas turns and crosses her arms. "Let me guess, you tried sliding into home plate, face-first."

The boy sniffles, then lowers his head and shakes it, sending all sorts of orange dust into the room. "First base," he reluctantly admits.

I'm about to ask if he was safe or out when I see Apá rounding the corner. He's wearing the same baggy gray sweats and Dodgers T-shirt from last night. Worse yet, he's got that familiar sleepy look, glassy red eyes and all.

I know that look. Saw it up close plenty of times until Amá got fed up and kicked him out.

Question is . . . does Ms. Ornelas see it too?

Apá comes over and wraps an arm around me, kisses me on the forehead—habits he only started doing again lately.

Orange-dirt boy has the nerve to actually chuckle. I try to play it off cool, like it's no big deal. But that all changes the second I get a whiff of him. There's no doubt about it—he's liquored up.

My stomach suddenly twists itself into a giant knot and I get a bad case of the shakes. It pretty much feels like the time I finished Amá's double espresso she'd left behind on the kitchen counter.

Jitters is what she called it.

And that's what I've got now . . . all over my entire

body. All I want to do now is find a way to get out of here as soon as possible.

Ms. Ornelas waves hi from across the room. Fortunately, she's too busy finding the correct-sized gauzes for the injured kid to properly greet Apá. "Hola, Señor Castillo. ¿Cómo has estado?"

"Muy bien," Apá answers with the slightest slur. He extends his hand and is about to approach her, when I pull him back. "Come on, Apá. We'd better get going. My stomach is starting to feel strange again."

Without missing a beat, Ms. Ornelas asks if I need to "visit" the bathroom before I go. I shake my head while leading Apá away again.

"Señor Castillo," Ms. Ornelas calls, "you have to sign Isaac out."

Great. We're just one good whiff away from having things turn bad real quick. So when Ms. Ornelas reaches for a pen from her NURSES DO ALL THE REAL WORK mug, I step in front of her and grab a pen myself. "It's okay, Ms. Ornelas. I got this," I say with my most polite smile.

I hand Apá the pen. The scent of alcohol seems to be filling the room.

Ms. Ornelas doesn't question my intent. "Oh . . .

thank you" is all she says. But that doesn't keep her from taking a step toward us.

Fortunately, that's when her walkie-talkie goes off. The school principal, Mrs. Carey, is reporting a girl with a sprained ankle and is asking for a wheelchair by the front quad. Ms. Ornelas excuses herself and rushes out a side door, pushing a wheelchair in front of her.

Finally, I can breathe again, which isn't so great when all you smell is alcohol.

MARCO
CHAPTER 12

The final bell rings. Just about everyone pulls out their phones and rushes the exit gate. So far, fortunately, I don't see anyone with frosted hair. I try to hurry, but it's really tough to do when I keep bruising the backs of kids' ankles with my ZÏPPA.

"Oops, sorry."

"Oh, excuse me."

"Sorry, my fault."

I'm literally running out of ways to apologize. My ZÏPPA's a real ankle killer.

My mom texts me that she's all the way at the back of the pickup line and lets me know that Isaac got picked up early. Poor guy. He pushed himself too hard trying to protect me.

Mrs. Carey stands by with her principal's walkie-talkie in hand, reminding all of us to make one single line, only no one listens.

The front steps are busier and noisier than the boys' locker room, but I don't really mind it. It makes it easier for someone as short as me to stay hidden.

I know that Nick and Ryan said they'd look out for me. But they can't walk me to each of my classes. And they definitely can't protect me from all the aggressives at this school. From all the running and shoving I'm seeing, there are just too many aggressives and semi-aggressives to even count.

I eventually reach the pickup line and take a seat on my ZĪPPA. The few kids around me are all hunch-backed with full backpacks. I catch them looking my way. I'm thinking they're wishing they had a ZĪPPA just about now.

A quick honk gets my attention. It's my mom driving up along the curb, with the side door sliding open. I leap in and pull the backpack into the middle seat before buckling up.

"So, mijo? How was it?" she asks while pulling away.

I feel a lump at the back of my throat but do my best to swallow it away. "Great, Mom."

I do as Isaac's abuelita always tells us and focus on the positive. She says negative thoughts should never be given that kind of power. Sometimes, I feel like she's my grandma too.

"You won't believe it," I tell Mom. "But I got my own nickname today."

"A nickname?" she asks with a bit of panic in her voice.

"Yep. And not just any nickname. A jock one!"

Her eyes grow huge. "Really? Well, don't keep me in suspense. What is it?"

"Mugs," I say proudly. "It's short for Muggsy Bogues. He's the smallest player to ever play in the NBA. A few friends invited me to try out for the team with them."

Mom makes a funny face. "That's . . . great, mijo. I didn't know you liked basketball."

"Yeah, me neither. But it sounds like a lot of fun. When I get home, I'm going to look up a few videos on how to play. There's a week before tryouts, so I'm pretty sure I can figure it out by then."

"You know, your father played basketball. His senior year, the team made all-state. He was team captain *and* MVP."

"Yes, Mom," I say. "You've mentioned it like a

thousand times." Only the way she's staring straight ahead, I'm not sure she hears a word I say.

"That's the day your father and I met—at the after-party. We danced for *hours*." Thankfully, she finally snaps out of it. "I could call and ask him to teach you a few things."

Mom does this a lot. Just about anything starts up her memories. Like me, she has a *play* button in her head.

I slide my backpack next to my feet and start thinking about the last time my dad came over to visit.

Isaac and I were in the kitchen, waiting for the cinnamon buns to bake. Dad came into the kitchen and asked what we were up to.

I pointed to the empty bag of flour and answered, "Making dessert, for dinner."

Dad just stood there and rolled his eyes, looking bothered. Only not as bothered as he was seeing the way I crossed my legs. Right there, in front of Isaac, he gave out a sort of guttural grunt and kicked my legs apart. "The least you could do," he said with a disgusted look on his face, "is sit like a man."

And just like that, he left . . . permanently.

Isaac did his best to change the subject, even

challenged me to a game of chess. It was the first and only time he ever beat me.

Now, before too long, Mom and I arrive at home. I go straight to my room and start my research. The amount of information is overwhelming. Did you know basketball was invented by a Canadian back in 1891?

I add the word "beginner" to the search. The number of videos seems limitless.

A few hours in, my mom knocks on the door and offers me dinner. Only I'm not hungry—well, for food anyway. I've got half my notepad filled with drills and plays that promise to turn me into a pro. I shut my eyes and try to visualize myself on the court, following through with my wrist on every pretend shot.

Honestly, the game doesn't seem that complicated. It's just a matter of tossing the ball into your opponent's basket more times than they do—not rocket science.

I roll up a pair of old socks and practice shooting them into my wastebasket. Five perfect shots later, I decide it's time for more of a challenge.

I stick my head out my window, but there's no sign of Isaac in his room. I know for a fact that he wouldn't mind me practicing on his driveway court. Mom, however, catches me on the way out and makes me gobble down a Costco chicken drumstick and a stalk of broccoli before I can leave the house.

I chew and swallow the food faster than even I can imagine. Mom seems surprised at my new appetite.

Fortunately for me, Isaac keeps a collection of basketballs in a bin by the side of his house. I pull out a multicolored one and practice dribbling it on the driveway.

Turns out that dribbling is a bit more difficult than it looks. The videos that I watched all say to use only the tips of your fingers. I try that, but it bends them back in a painful kind of way.

Again, I close my eyes and picture shooting a perfect shot. I can't help but picture a whole crowd too, cheering. And Dad in the middle, holding up a sign with my name on it. Maybe even my new nickname.

I know exactly what I have to do. I mean, a few crooked fingers never hurt anyone, right?

One dribble, two dribbles, and jump. Okay, now it's time to add a shot to that routine.

One dribble, two dribbles, jump *and* shoot. The ball soars but falls short. I walk up underneath, wondering if it's regulation height. The rims on the videos don't look anywhere near as high.

Well, they say Rome wasn't built in a day. So I can't expect to be as good as Isaac after a few hours. I've got to keep going. Who knows? Maybe by the end of the week, I'll surprise Isaac and challenge him to a one-on-one game.

First, though, I need to make one basket and go from there.

ISAAC
CHAPTER 13

As we step outside, I spot a school police officer pulling alongside the yellow drop-off curb. Apá doesn't even seem to notice. A few weeks ago, Amá made me promise never to get into a car with him if he's been drinking. But I can't say no right now. Can't risk causing a scene and getting him in trouble. Maybe arrested. I stay quiet and climb into the front seat of his Tacoma truck. I buckle my seat belt and, from there, watch the officer enter the school.

Apá gets into his seat, turns on the radio. "¿Listo?"

Again, I lie. "Yeah, ready." I squeeze down and brace myself as Apá presses on the gas pedal. He's got his favorite CD playing. A collection of sixties rock. It's been a while since I've heard it, so I don't remember the lyrics. Apá does. He's singing along, something he never does, at least not when he's sober.

"Mijo, you feeling okay? We can stop somewhere and get some food." His eyes widen with excitement, making them extra glassy. "How 'bout Don Francisco's?" he asks. "You can get some of those cheese fries you love."

Apá's right. I do love those fries. They're cut extra wide and are double fried so that the cheese doesn't make them all soggy. Then they sprinkle the whole plate with bacon bits. Tons and tons of bacon bits.

Only I can't. Not with Apá inching his way into the right bike lane. The idea of him getting pulled over and arrested scares me. But the idea of him accidentally hitting and killing someone freaks me out even more. I've got to get him off the road as soon as possible! I love my Apá, but I can't let him ruin his life . . . or anyone else's.

"No thanks, Apá. I'm good. I don't want to risk throwing up again."

"We can get you a soda," he answers in a singsong voice.

A mandarin-flavored Jarritos is exactly what my stomach needs. Don Francisco's is only a few blocks away. But that's just me thinking with my belly. "Nuh, Apá," I finally say. "I just need to get a bit of rest."

He reaches over and feels my forehead. His hand is

so rough and warm, I don't know how they'd ever be able to sense anything.

"You feel okay. Want me to drive you to your mom's house?"

Your mom's house. I hate the way that sounds. Not too long ago, it used to be *ours*. Only now, it doesn't feel like anyone's anymore.

And that's another reason I can't let him drive me there. Amá's made it perfectly clear: Apá is welcome to come over, welcome to come and see me . . . as long as he is sober.

She threatened to take him to court and fight for full custody if he ever broke that rule.

I know Apá's not perfect. I know he needs help. But I don't want to lose him either. So having him drop me off is a bad idea. What if Amá came home early and approached him?

She's seen him drunk enough times that she can pretty much tell if he's been drinking simply by looking into his eyes. I'm not sure exactly how she does it, but I can't take the chance.

"Actually, Apá," I say with my head down, "could we go to your apartment? I think I need to use the restroom." This time, it's no longer a lie. I really am feeling sick. Really do need to visit the bathroom.

Apá looks disappointed. Today was his day off—probably a drinking day—and here I am, ruining his plans.

He glances over at me with his glassy red eyes, most likely trying to find a good excuse not to take me with him.

It's not all his fault. He's been really down this whole year. It all started after Apá's dad died of some sort of cancer. Apá barely mentioned him when he was alive, but said even less after he passed. In fact, Apá stayed mostly quiet . . . just disappeared into the garage to do "woodwork."

Then things got worse. His sister passed away too—from a stroke. *Her,* I do remember. My Tía Esperanza was real nice too. Even though I didn't see her too often, she always remembered me and brought me back T-shirts from every place she traveled. Vegas. Egypt. Cancún. It didn't matter.

She gave the biggest hugs too. I'll never forget the way she'd reach around me and smoosh my face against her chest. I'd cringe and hold my breath, but the mixture of perfume and that same pink lotion Abuelita uses, too, will always stick with me.

She was the oldest by nine years, and according to what Apá once told me, she pretty much raised him. Her death shocked everyone. Especially him. The stroke hit her in the middle of the night. It was as unexpected as it was cruel.

Apá didn't handle it well. I'd never seen him such a mess. Sometimes, I'd wake up and hear him stumbling around in the kitchen. I'd sneak out of my room and catch him in just his underwear, going into the "secret" stash of liquor he kept hidden over the refrigerator.

It was so different from when Amá's Apá died. Both deaths came only weeks apart. Losing my abuelito was tough too. The difference was we all knew it was happening. We all got to spend time with him. Got to say our goodbyes.

Maybe that's what bothered Apá. He never got to say anything to his sister, never got one last hug.

After that, he and Amá started having problems.

If Apá went too much time without a drink, he'd start acting all grumpy and antsy, like he couldn't stand being home. Drinking had pretty much become more important than either Amá or me.

Then he'd say he needed to go outside for air and disappear for a few hours, coming home really late at night.

That's when the arguing would start. Somehow, my name always came up . . . which really sucked. Wish he could be happy with just Amá and me, and not need the drinking.

One day, though, after a long, long talk with Amá, he promised never to drink in front of me. Something about not wanting me to end up like him. At first, I was pretty happy about it. But later, after seeing a lot less of him, I started wondering if having a liquored-up Apá around was better than not having him around at all.

Downtown is up ahead. I can see the federal building towering above Apá's apartment complex. Apá cuts a sharp right and pulls in as he pushes the automatic garage opener. Finally, we come to a complete stop. *Thank God.*

Apá parks so crookedly that I can barely squeeze out from my side. I brush past his built-in woodshop area but can't spot a single tool, just a pile of boxes stacked on top of each other.

Apá opens the door leading upstairs to his apartment. He has this thing about always racing me upstairs, something about proving that he is still young and in shape. Not this time, though. The thought of racing doesn't seem to enter his mind.

Eventually, we get to the second floor, the

93

living-room-kitchen area.

"Don't mind the tiliche," he says. "I haven't had a chance to clean up."

Forget the mess, I can't keep my eyes off the monstrous TV that just about covers an entire wall. "Oh my God. How big is that TV?"

Apá tries to play it cool. "Eighty-four inches. It's 4K *and* UHD."

I lean in closer and touch the sound bar. "What's UHD?"

Apá shrugs. "Who knows? But it looks amazing." He reaches for the bedsheet covering his couch and yanks it away. "You're going to love this."

I run my hand across the leather couch and take in the new-leather scent. "Isn't all this really expensive?"

"Un poquito," he says. "I thought this way you'd want to come over and visit."

"Of course I want to visit . . . but not 'cause of all this."

"I know, mijo. It's just that I messed things up and wanted to make it up to you. I figured we could make nachos and catch a few movies when you stay over." He pushes the coffee table forward. "Come here, check this out." Apá lets himself fall back onto the couch, reaches over to a knob on the side, and reclines back. Way back.

A *reclining couch!* I can barely believe my eyes.

"Claro que sí," he says. "I'd been wanting a couch like this forever. But your mother wouldn't let me. Said it was too bulky, too feo. It's Italian leather. I got a great price on a floor model."

I sink into place and gotta admit, it's super comfortable. I can already picture myself lying back with a bag of popcorn, watching scary movies that Amá won't let me see at home.

"You thirsty?" Apá asks, while already heading toward the kitchen.

"A little bit," I say, following behind. "Do you have any soda?"

Apá's fridge catches me off guard. It's new and super fancy, with four doors. He swings the middle doors open. One side is stacked high with juice pouches, while the other is crammed full with boxed Lunchables.

"Told you I've been getting this place ready for you." Apá ruffles my hair and smiles. "Is your stomach up for a snack?"

I smile back. "Yes, Apá. My stomach's doing much better now."

MARCO

CHAPTER 14

Okay. Basketball is way tougher to play than I thought. According to my watch, I've been out here practicing for almost two hours. Except for two really close shots, I've made zero baskets. Zero. A big fat serote, like Isaac always jokes.

Most of my shots fall short and slam against the garage door. The rest ricochet off either the backboard or the front of the rim, which of course doesn't get you a point.

I could really use some help, but when I go to the front door and ask for Isaac, his mom tells me he's with his dad but doesn't know when he'll be home, since neither one of them is answering their phones.

"Mijo"—she looks at me holding my throbbing

middle finger—"what happened?"

I hold up my right hand. "It's no big deal. I just jammed my finger. Isaac says injuries are like badges of honor and that only real ballers wear them." I look at it closely, just now realizing how swollen it's gotten. It hurts like crazy.

Isaac's mom shakes her head. "Qué locuras. Where do you kids come up with those crazy ideas? Come on in, mijo. We'd better ice it before it swells any further."

I take a seat at the kitchen table and soak my finger in the cup of ice and sea salt, watching as she grills up a cheese sandwich for me. That's the thing about Isaac's mom, she's always looking to feed people. Especially me. It's like she thinks it'll help me grow or something.

After eating the most delicious grilled three-cheese sandwich ever, I go back to practice my driving in, something the videos say Muggsy Bogues was the best at. He could go up against the tallest of players and finish off with this thing called a finger roll. So far, I've got the move memorized.

I back up all the way to the curb and remind myself to count my steps aloud. Okay, here I go.

One. Two. Only the ball flies out of my hands as I go for my shot. The ball clanks off the bottom of the rim and bounces back to me, clonking me right smack in the face before rolling down the driveway and into the street.

Shooting with my left hand makes the drill way tougher. I'm not sure, but I might be spending more time on the street chasing down the ball than I do on the court.

Still, I can't give up. Muggsy would never do that. Online, people called Muggsy pesty and feisty. That's what I've got to become. And practice is the only way to do it—even if it means more swollen fingers.

So I try again.

And again.

And again.

And . . . well, you get the picture.

Another good hour passes when *my* mom comes out to check on me. She bends down and picks up my latest miss. Then, with both hands, she dribbles closer to the basket and launches the ball. Her shot hits the rectangle target on the backboard and bounces in. *Two points!*

She pumps her arms in the air and circles around me while hooting.

I run after the rebound and dribble with my back turned to her so that she can't see my eyes welling up.

Only I think she figures it out with some sort of mom power.

"It was just beginner's luck," she answers.

Beginner's luck? I start to wonder where mine is. Only, I'm not about to say this to her. "Good shot, Mom." There's no point making her feel bad simply for being better at this than me. "I didn't know you knew how to play."

"I don't. It's the first shot I've ever taken."

My heart winces, feeling like someone purple-nurpled me inside.

"But I did watch your father play dozens of times."

"It's okay, Mom," I say, taking a seat on the ball. "Maybe I just wasn't made for this."

"Anything I can do to help?"

My mind races. "Well, maybe there is. Dad's always wanted to see me play a sport. Could you ask him to teach me how to play basketball?"

Mom bites her lower lip. Her hesitation tells me everything I need to know.

"I don't know . . . you know how busy he is with work."

Mom is good at so many things, but covering up for Dad isn't one of them.

"It's okay. I'll just figure it out myself." Suddenly, my finger doesn't bother me at all.

I back up to the crack Isaac uses as the free-throw line, making sure to bend my knees and extend my arm as I shoot. It's a perfect rainbow. Perfect arc. Perfect spin.

The perfect air ball.

ISAAC
CHAPTER 15

It's eight o'clock by the time Apá gets me home to Amá. I run inside, calling for her.

"Amá! Amá! You'll never believe the size of Apá's new TV. That thing is huge! And the sound, it's amazing. Just like—"

Finally, I track her down. She's sitting at the kitchen table, her head resting on her elbow. Next to her are two untouched plates. The potatoes are smothered in gravy so dry that it reminds me of that fondant frosting they use to decorate those fancy cakes on TV.

Uh-oh. I know the look she's giving me. Amá doesn't say a word. She doesn't have to. I know I'm in trouble.

"Mijo," Apá says, coming up from behind me. "You forgot your . . . backpack."

Amá gives Apá the very same look. Apparently, we're *both* in trouble. Fortunately, Apá has sobered up enough to get past Amá's powerful radar.

Amá turns back to me with a clenched smile. "Oh, hi. Nice of you to finally make it home."

Then she reaches for a fork and stabs one of the unsuspecting mounds of mashed potatoes. The gravy and potatoes have been sitting for so long that they crack and split down the middle. Amá's Spanish accent comes out a bit whenever she's upset. Apá calls it her Latina temper. Whatever it is, I can hear a bit of it now.

"I picked up some carnitas and spent a good hour making that special gravy you love so much. After your first day of middle school, I thought you might appreciate it. Guess I was wrong."

Apá and I glance at one another, each of us taking a deep breath.

"I'm sorry, Amá," I say. It's not something I say just to get Apá and me out of trouble. It's something I definitely mean. Problem is, Amá's heard it a million times. So I'm not sure it's worth much.

"It's just that I had two Lunch . . . ables." Unfortunately, I catch myself too late. I swear, I could smack myself right about now.

I sneak a peek at Apá. He's shaking his head.

"Lunch-a-bles?" Amá extends the words into three long syllables, and I think I know what's coming next. Only this time, she pans her scowl to both of us. "It's past eight o'clock. Those must have been some big boxes."

"No, Amá," I say trying to help Apá, "we watched a movie and played some—" This time, I think it's Apá who wants to smack me.

"Look, Vero." His voice is especially sharp—something I never heard until this year. "I was simply showing him my new electronics. You know, for when he visits."

Amá's accent is getting thicker each second. "No, I don't know. Because I was here going through all the school emails and trying to figure out how to set up"—she starts holding up her fingers—"my parent portal, Aeries account, Dojo, Seesaw, and all the other crazy apps teachers require of us. Key word . . . us!" Amá's accent goes about as thick as it ever gets. She's upset. Really upset.

Apá lowers his head. I feel bad for him—I know exactly how he feels. I mean, it isn't like he's not trying. It's just that with Amá, trying isn't good enough. Don't get me wrong, I'm not trying to put the blame on her either.

I just wish she'd understand. Apá and I are wired differently than her, maybe with a few wires crossed here and there. I'm not sure. "Amá, it's not his fault. I—" Only she raises a finger and just like that, my turn to speak is over.

"You did check his agenda, right? *And* each syllabus his teachers sent home. Right?" The second "right" comes with an added look.

Suddenly, Apá turns on me. Whenever Amá gets mad like this, it automatically becomes every man for himself.

"Look, don't blame me. I didn't know he had any homework." He turns my way. "Isaac, you didn't tell me about any of these things."

Isaac? Wow, I *am* on my own. Apá never calls me that. It's always "Mijo this," or "Mijo that." Talk about trying to distance himself from me. It's a new low, if you ask me.

"It's your responsibility, not mine," he continues. "I went through middle school and high school *and* two years of junior college without anyone watching over me. Your amá and I aren't always going to be around to take care of you. You need to be your own man. Take care of *your* obligations."

My mind shifts through the few classes I did make it through today before puking. Homeroom–language arts, science, and PE. There's no point in going for my agenda. I already know it's blank.

"I'm sorry, Amá. I guess I forgot . . . again." It's the *again* that hurts most on the way out.

Amá takes a deep breath. "Look, mijo." At the very least, her gentle tone is back. "It was the first day of school—we can't have a repeat of last year. You almost failed fifth grade."

She reaches for me and holds my hand. "I need you to try harder."

Harder? I'm not sure I can.

And that's when the room goes quiet. Part of me wishes someone would just start yelling at me so I could get the lecture out of the way. But Amá goes over to Apá, pats his shoulder, and gestures toward the living room. "Mijo, why don't you go to your room and get those forms we need to sign? Your Apá and I need to talk."

There's no need to guess how this plays out. They're gonna go in there and talk about me. Come up with a "strategy" to help me succeed.

Back in my room, I fling my backpack onto my corner

desk and let myself fall back onto my bed. I wonder if they'd say the same things if they knew I could hear them plenty clear from here.

Three. Two. One.

"Why do I always have to play the villain?" Amá argues.

There it is. The bickering has started.

"Don't you think I want to have fun with him too?" Amá asks, almost pleading. "But I can't. He's got eight different classes this year. Six different teachers. I don't know how to get him through this."

Ouch!

Judging from Apá's silence, those words hit him plenty hard too.

After a few seconds, Amá continues. "Mira, Viejo." *Viejo?* That's her go-to nickname for Apá. I haven't heard that in forever. "I'm grateful that you picked him up. I know you're always ready to drop everything for him. And I love you for that. But there's a lot more to raising a son than that. He doesn't need a friend. He needs a father."

I'm not sure how Apá's going to handle this, but after another bit of silence, he clears his throat. "Mira, Vero . . . I was caught off guard. That's all. I've been working really hard to get myself cleaned up. Working really hard to be sure that Junior wants to come over." Suddenly, his voice starts to break and I realize that he's actually crying. "I don't want to lose him. He's all I've got left. Maybe I did go overboard with the TV and video games. But I promise, I'll make sure he gets his homework done from now on."

I wipe a tear from the corner of my eye.

"Okay, Viejo. And while you're at it, could you have a talk with your son about forgetting to wear deodorant? Pobre niño is starting to smell like day-old cheeseburger."

Cheeseburger? I lift my arm and take a whiff. Great. She's right about that too!

"Okay," Apá says. "Tell Junior I said goodbye." And just like that, I hear the front door closing. Once again, Apá's gone.

The correct thing to do would be to shower and rub the cheeseburger smell off my pits. But that's the least of my problems. My head feels like it weighs a thousand pounds as I think back to PE class, back to me racing those two eighth graders, pushing myself so hard that I actually puked.

Ama's right. I *can* try harder. I need to do better. I'm

going to study so hard that Amá might confuse me for Marco.

Of course, that's when my phone goes off. I do my best to ignore the buzz, but it won't stop.

I peel myself up and reach for my phone. It's a text from Marco:

Little pig, little pig. It's a running joke Marco and I have.

I go over to my window. Sure enough, Marco's standing outside with his sweaty face pressed up against the glass.

MARCO

CHAPTER 16

It takes a while, but Isaac eventually comes to the window, rubbing pretend hairs over his lower jaw. "Not by the hair on my chinny chin chin!"

I tuck my phone back into my pocket. "Then I will huff and I will puff and I will blow your house down!" I take a monster breath and blow across his window, fogging up a tiny circle.

Isaac cracks a smile and cranks open the window.

Without my ZÏPPA to stand on, I've got no choice but to hold out my hand for help getting in. Unfortunately, I forget about my finger and Isaac squeezes at the worst spot possible.

I yelp instinctively.

Isaac lets go, sending me crashing onto the ground below.

He sticks his head out the window. "Dude, you all right?"

"Yeah," I say, a little embarrassed, but mostly disappointed. I'd been anxious to show off my "baller badge" to him, but *this* wasn't the way I'd imagined it.

Again, Isaac offers me a hand.

This time, I reach out with my good hand.

"What happened?" he asks.

"I jammed my finger while practicing."

"Practicing what?"

"Basketball, of course," I say, holding it out for him to see.

He instantly makes a face. "Dude, that's pretty bad."

I smile. "Baller badge, right?"

"Heck, yeah!" he says, nodding. "That's gotta be painful, though?"

"Yeah, good thing it was a finger I never use," I say, taking a seat at the edge of his bed. "How are *you* doing? I came over to make sure you were good."

His head drops. "I still can't believe I puked on Mr. Chavez. On the first day!"

"It happens. How's your stomach doing? Any diarrhea?" I ask.

Isaac shakes his head. "Dude, what is it with people and diarrhea?"

"What?" I say, shrugging. "It's normal. Nothing bad."

"Nothing good either."

"Anyway, thanks for looking out for me," I say.

"Dude, it's no big deal."

"Yeah . . . it is." I sigh. "But that's not why I came over."

"Let me guess, you heard my parents arguing too."

I nod.

"How much did you hear?"

"Not much."

Isaac side-eyes me.

"Okay. I heard most of it. Want to talk about it?"

Isaac sighs before digging into his hamper and pulling out a T-shirt, which he crumples into a tight ball. "No, not really," he says, shooting the makeshift ball at a miniature hoop over his door. A perfect swish.

I get up and dig into his hamper too. Thankfully, I pull out a tank top, which ends up about a foot short of its target. "Seriously, Isaac."

Again, he gives me a look. "It's personal."

"Personal?" I dig for another shirt from his hamper. "You had no trouble telling me all about your blue poop after you downed a giant blue slushie," I say. "That's only because I was a bit worried about there being something wrong with me."

"So," I ask. "You need to talk?"

Isaac shakes his head, then lets himself fall back onto the bed, letting out an extra-long sigh.

I lie beside him as if we were on the couch, watching cartoons.

It takes a moment, but Isaac finally gets his words out. I reach over and squeeze his shoulder.

His voice is trembly. I can't tell if he's more angry or sad. Either way, it's impressive that he can hold it together. I can't help but be a bit jealous, because holding back emotions doesn't come so easy for me.

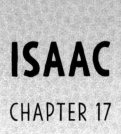

ISAAC

CHAPTER 17

Amá started taking me to a therapist after she and Apá first separated. Only I never really felt comfortable talking to him. Dr. Reynolds was nice and all, but he was no Marco.

You see, Marco has something that makes him even more qualified than a therapist with a Harvard degree—and that's a father who can't keep a promise either.

One difference, though, is that Marco's dad is barely around—if that.

Not that Marco's mom didn't try. In fact, back in third grade, she even made him a special offer. Spend time with Marco and avoid alimony and child support.

Dude actually chose to write a check. I know, right?

Guess that's the difference between our dads: *his*

doesn't bother pretending to care. This might be why Marco and I are so close. Brothers, really. There's nothing we can't tell each other.

I shut my eyes and do my best to speak, only my words are lodged tight at the back of my throat. Fortunately, Marco doesn't pressure me in any way.

"It hurts—" The words come out in a raspy whisper.

I try again. "It hurts to be such a disappointment."

Marco rolls over and squeezes my shoulder. "Yes . . . it does."

Like I said, this homie's like a brother to me. There's nothing we can't tell each other.

When we're done talking, Marco offers to help me go over my to-do list for tomorrow—even tries to sell me on the idea of getting a ZÏPPA like his.

I'm so desperate to do better that I almost agree.

The next morning, I get up without delay. I'm careful not to step on the clothes Marco laid out for me. Both the pants and shirt were Christmas presents I got in the mail from one of my many aunts in México. They've been sitting in my closet for months with all their tags still intact.

Neither piece is my style, but I can't imagine

114

disappointing Marco. Not after he stayed up late helping me. Thanks to him, I've got all my signed school forms, along with tons of neatly packed pencils, pens, and highlighters—and just about every size Post-it note imaginable.

Believe it or not, I'm actually looking forward to going back to school. Only it's got nothing to do with the crazy clothes I'm sporting. It's more about proving myself to Amá by going to class and filling out my agenda *each* and *every* period, just like every teacher asked. It might seem dumb, but I need to prove to Amá that I finally have my act together.

I make my way to the kitchen, where I find Abuelita hugging Amá, no doubt handing out that famous Abuelita wisdom of hers.

Amá reaches for her coffee, simultaneously wiping away her tears.

Abuelita is quick to notice my clothes and whistles loud enough for the entire neighborhood to hear. "Pero qué guapo muchacho."

I blush, but go ahead and spin around for them anyway.

Amá chimes in as well. "Trying to impress anyone in particular?"

"Nooooo . . . I'm just changing things up a bit. That's all," I say.

Amá hands me a plate of her famous bacon-avocado omelet, served up exactly like at her restaurant. It's steaming hot with melted cheese stacked up high. "Mijo, you think we could talk for a moment?"

Abuelita excuses herself and heads back to her room with a bagel and coffee on a tray attached to her walker.

I look over at Amá and nod.

I'm hoping it has nothing to do with what happened last night, but there's no way of avoiding it. We take our seats at the table, Amá with her coffee in hand, watching me struggle to squeeze the last bit of ketchup out of the plastic bottle. A few fart sounds later, my omelet is looking like a crime scene from one of those shows she watches when she thinks I'm not looking.

Amá takes a sip and lowers her WORLD'S BEST MOM mug I gave her for Mother's Day. "Mira, I know that spending time with your father is important to you. It's important to me too. He is a good man. Loves you more than anything else. But, mijo, you know as well as I do that he's been struggling."

She reaches for her coffee and takes another sip.

I take a bite of my omelet. It's still hot and burns

my mouth, but it also keeps me from saying anything about Apá being liquored up. I know it's pretty much the same as lying to Amá, but I know what would happen if I told her. And I can't bear the thought of not being able to see Apá anymore.

"I'm not so sure your father is in a place to help you with your responsibilities, not when he's struggling to deal with his."

This time, I go for a long gulp of milk. Anything to avoid looking her in the eye.

"Mijo. You know I still love your father, right?"

I let my eyes meet hers and nod.

She does her best to smile, but I can see Apá's problems weighing down at the corners of her mouth. I'd give anything to see her smile light up a room again, like it did back when things between her and Apá were good.

Amá cups the back of my hand with hers. "Okay, amor. We better get ready for school."

I do my best to smile back, but the ends of *my* mouth feel way heavy too.

I go to the bathroom to wash my hands. Fortunately, Abuelita's not in here this morning. I look myself over in the bathroom mirror, check out my new look. It's definitely not me. I yank the shirt out of my pants and roll up the sleeves—way better.

Believe it or not, I'm actually ready before Marco. I wait for his mom and him in their driveway while repeatedly reminding myself aloud to fill out my agenda today.

When we get to school, things go pretty much the same way they did yesterday. Difference is . . . I'm not nervous at all. I'm not focused on fitting in or looking cool. All I want from the day is to stay focused long enough to get my work done and earn good grades—to make Amá proud.

Could it be my new attitude? Whatever it is, this morning, I don't mind having to wait as Marco hugs his mom like he's never going to see her again. I don't mind his jazz hands waving goodbye or the sight of his rolling backpack bumping into kids as he hauls it along.

Maybe it's the new clothes Marco picked out for me? Maybe it's all the work Marco and I put in last night? I'm not sure, but whatever it is, it definitely feels good.

My newfound swag continues way after Marco and I go our separate ways to our classes, which are cut a bit short today because of modified schedule, meaning we go to all our classes on account of teachers needing to meet or something. My swag holds as I pass through the lunch-area stairway, where eighth-grade boys and girls glare at anybody going by. Only, it pretty much vanishes entirely when I step into Ms. Kempe's class and Dos Equis takes a seat beside me. The dude's like way shorter than me, almost half a foot, and yet, he acts like he's six feet tall.

I try to ignore him as he hands out high fives, only it's tough to do when he's so loud.

"Hey, man . . . bring it here," he says to some kid two desks over.

"Bro," the boy answers as he walks over and side-hugs him. "Long time no see."

Are you kidding me? How is anyone buying any of this?

I reach into my backpack and pull out my agenda. Dos Equis is *not* about to distract me from getting it filled in. I grab my No. 2 pencil, but the tip Marco worked so hard to sharpen has broken off. I scour the room for a sharpener. At the back of the room, Ms. Kempe has one of those old-school crank ones.

It definitely fits her style.

I turn the lever as fast as my hand can go, until the pencil tip is so sharp that it looks more like a needle.

Ms. Kempe is on the phone, laughing like only she can.

"Hey, Isaac." It's Dos Equis, standing behind me.

His voice sounds sincere enough that for a split second I think he might apologize for having called Marco a dork.

"Hey," I say back.

Dos Equis glances over at Ms. Kempe, making sure the coast is clear. He reaches into his back pocket, pulls out his phone, and swipes past a few screens.

"Remember that thing I said about you having to worry about your reputation?"

I nod, mostly out of curiosity.

"Well, forget it." He holds up his phone to me. I see a video of me throwing up on Mr. Chavez's feet. "I'm pretty sure your rep is set in stone."

Dumb me just sits there, staring at the phone . . . speechless.

"At least it will be," he says, smirking, "after I post this video."

Just then, panic sets in and I reach over for his phone, only Dos Equis leans back. I'm not about to let him get away with this. I manage to grab onto the phone, only my off hand pushes him harder than planned, causing him to lose his balance and fall backward over some kid's desk. I cringe as I watch him flip upside down as if doing a cartwheel.

The entire class turns and laughs—everyone except for Ms. Kempe, who puts down her own phone and rushes over.

Dos Equis is holding his foot, grimacing.

Ms. Kempe takes the phone from me and asks me what happened. I think about telling her the truth. But that would mean getting Dos Equis in trouble over the video—and I definitely don't want to be *that* kid. You know . . . the one who goes to the teacher and snitches.

Ms. Kempe asks the kids around us if they saw what happened. Luckily, they all just shrug.

Suddenly, the kids around us gasp as Dos Equis finally sits up. HIS. FOOT. IS. LITERALLY. DANGLING!

I can't believe it. I've never hurt anyone before . . . well, not unless you count second grade—but that was different.

Margo Silvia had it coming. I warned her plenty of times that I didn't like to be tickled. Punching her in the nose was a total reflex. A few more seconds and

I would have peed right there in the middle of class. This, however, *was* my fault. *I* let my emotions get the better of me.

Ms. Kempe drops down to one knee and asks Dos Equis if he's okay, which seems like an odd question to ask someone who obviously just broke a bone.

I look down at him, expecting him to spill the beans.

He snorts back a bit of snot and looks up at me.

My heart races. With my record, I'll probably be facing a suspension, maybe worse. What's Amá gonna say? How is she gonna react?

Dos Equis finally breaks the uncomfortable silence. "I was just leaning back," he says, grimacing with clenched teeth. "Guess I went back too far."

Ms. Kempe gives me a questioning look. It's clear she isn't buying his story, but without a confession, there's really nothing she can do other than get Dos Equis some help. "Okay, then. Let's have the nurse come and get you. Looks like you'll need to visit the emergency room."

Ms. Kempe heads back to her desk to make the call, and I lean over and try apologizing to Dos Equis. Only he's not having any of it and is ignoring me completely.

A few minutes later, Ms. Ornelas arrives with a

wheelchair and rolls out with Dos Equis.

I keep to myself the rest of the period. Ms. Kempe tries to lighten the mood with her best jokes, but even they fail to crack my scowl.

All period long, I think about what I did.

The thought stays with me way after the bell rings, way after I take a seat in Mr. Widén's class. Fortunately, he's having us do a virtual frog dissection on school iPads, which, at the very least, gets the other kids to stop talking about what happened.

MARCO

CHAPTER 18

My phone rings. Believe it or not, Isaac is up before me. I know I should get up and get ready for school, but I'm super sleepy. I feel like a leaky balloon trying to hold itself up—except for my right middle finger, of course. It's bruised and swollen in the middle as if pumped full of air.

I glance over at Isaac through his bedroom window. Of course he's busy playing hoops with his hamper. The boy eats, sleeps, and breathes basketball. Only, I can tell by the way he's missing every shot that his parents' arguing is bothering him.

It's kind of ironic though, you know, that he tells *me* about it. Especially when I'd give anything to be more like him. Back in elementary school, he was all anyone seemed to talk about—especially the girls. They'd hand me notes in class, asking me questions about him.

What his favorite color was.

His favorite soda.

And who he liked.

But Isaac just played it cool. He'd smile and wave at everyone, which only made the girls like him even more.

But it's not just girls who like him. Heck, everyone does. What's there not to like?

Isaac has the best hair. It's messy and just kind of curls down onto his face, only in a cool way, not like mine.

And don't get me started on his muscles, which seemed to have appeared overnight. Seriously, Isaac looks like an "after" picture of me for some miracle growth formula ad. Whenever he wears a tank top, the muscles all seem to move around on their own.

When *I* try to wear one, the straps slip right off; one of the many problems of having shoulders as broad as a wire hanger.

Honestly, Isaac could be best friends with anyone at school. I'm not sure why he settles for me.

Again, my phone vibrates. It's my backup alarm. What can I say? I like to play it safe. *Really* safe.

I pick it up and stare at the same screen from last night, Dad's social media page. It's the reason I couldn't sleep last night. After climbing in from Isaac's house, I made the mistake of checking on my dad's activities. I know it sounds dumb, but it somehow makes me feel like part of his life.

Dad's added a few more photos since last night. More pics of him and his girlfriend, along with her son, *Sean*. The three of them are at the beach, tossing a Frisbee.

I zoom in on Dad's face. He's smiling like he's never been happier. They all are. The woman. And *Sean*. Smiles for miles. The photo looks like the kind that comes free with the frame.

Honestly, it feels like a bad dream. Only it's real.

I swipe my phone quiet with my good finger. You'd think I would know better.

There's a knock at my door. "Mijo, are you up?" It's my mom, making a rare wake-up call.

I fling my phone aside. "Yes, Mom."

She comes in anyway and asks to see my finger. Her eyes squint, then go wide as she examines it closely.

"¡Pobrecito! We'd better take you to the doctor."

"Mom, I'm fine. It's just a little swollen."

She shoots me a look. "Swollen is what happens to my feet after a day of wearing high heels. This is more than that. I'm calling the doctor's office to make an appointment."

"*Mom*," I say, dragging out the word. Only she's got mom tunnel vision and wouldn't notice an airplane landing in our yard right now.

With that, I head toward the bathroom to shower. I strip down to my underwear, and I brush my teeth while the water warms.

Then, just as the mirror in front of me is starting to fog, I stand up straight, and using a good finger, I draw a perfect six-pack on my reflection like Isaac's.

Mom tells me to be patient. That things will change once puberty starts. Only I can't wait much longer.

The only real lines on my belly are my fold lines from when I sit down.

I raise both arms and lean in closer to the mirror to check my pits. That's when I find it. One long straggly hair sticking to the side.

I immediately reach for it, trying to straighten it out so I can better estimate its full length. Only as I try to hold it, the tiny fellow sticks against my finger.

I roll it between my fingers and watch it dissolve.

Figures it would just be a bit of lint.

Oscar, Jorge, and Orlando rush over to me the second I enter the school drop-off area.

"Marco!" hollers Orlando. "You won't believe it. Ms. Cabrera, the robotics club adviser, said we could start meeting after school to build our robot for the Robotics Invitational Challenge."

"Yeah," adds Oscar, "she told us it's a one-day tournament against all the other schools. With huge trophies for the winner."

Orlando cuts back in. "Ms. Cabrera says we can start building . . . as long as we find a fourth group member."

Jorge doesn't say much, just nods.

"I'd love to," I start to say as Orlando high-fives Oscar and Jorge. "But I can't. I've got to get ready for basketball tryouts."

Orlando's forehead wrinkles like he's trying to make sense of what I just said.

Finally, Jorge speaks. "Basketball?"

"Yep. I'm gonna play point guard."

Orlando gives me a confused look. "Um, no offense, but aren't you a bit short to play basketball?"

I laugh as we start walking to class. "Too short? No way." I pull out my phone to show them a clip of Muggsy.

"Dude!" Orlando scrunches his face. "What happened to your finger?"

I hold it up high enough for everyone to see. "Oh, this. No biggie, just part of the game, you know." (Something I heard online.)

"You can't play with your finger like that," says Oscar, all cringy-faced.

I've seen Isaac play with his fingers taped together. I'm sure I can do the same. "Anyway, here . . . you guys gotta see this," I say, changing the topic.

I show them a few Muggsy Bogues highlights but stop just as we enter Mr. Slaughter's classroom.

Oscar looks on, almost hypnotized. "That Muggsy guy is amazing!"

"Yep. And get this, he's only five foot three."

"Well, that's totally cool, Marco," says Orlando. "I never would have guessed you played ball too."

This is starting to sound so completely real that I can't help but smile. "Some of the guys trying out even gave me my very own on-court nickname."

"Dude, really?" Orlando seems more excited about it than me. "What is it?"

"Yeah," add Oscar and Jorge.

"MUGS," I say nice and loud. I might not live up to the name just yet, but give me a week. Muggsy Bogues himself would be proud.

Right then, Mr. Slaughter interrupts, handing me a slip. "Here you go, Mugs," he says with a grin.

It's a pupil release slip with the *Dr. Appt* box checked off. Guess Mom was able to get an appointment for me.

"Sorry, guys . . . Looks like I gotta go."

It might seem weird, but I'm actually looking forward to this visit. I've got a few questions for Dr. Osburn.

Dr. Stephen Osburn's examining room is *exactly* the same year after year. Same tan wallpaper. Same bulletin board covered in baby photos and postcards. Same exam table. Same exact copy of *Clifford the Big Red Dog* he had me read to him when I was four.

I even recognize the chewed-on corner. No, not my handiwork. I don't think.

Anyway, it's the first in the series, when Clifford won't stop growing until at the end when . . . never mind, I wouldn't want to spoil the ending. But trust me, it's good.

I carefully search the bulletin board for an old photo

130

of me. There I am, down at the bottom corner, with me in the doctor's arms, tugging away at his beard.

Except for the whole diaper thing, I look practically the same.

Mom searches the board too, oohing and aahing at all the cute faces.

Finally, the doctor knocks and enters with a smile. "Marco, how's my favorite patient doing?"

Yep. He's a total community fish. Super nice.

"I'm doing well," I say.

It's been a year since I last saw him. Part of me is hoping he might say something about how much taller I've gotten, but that's okay. I mean, who wants a doctor who lies, right?

Instead, he takes a seat at his computer and rubs his furry chin as he goes over the information the nurse collected from Mom and me when we first arrived.

He scoots his rolling stool up to me. "All right now, let's see that finger."

I hold it up and wince each time he bends or squeezes it.

"Is it okay?" I ask.

Dr. Osburn rolls back to the computer. "I'm pretty sure it's simply an acute contusion, but I'm going to have you get some X-rays. Just in case."

Acute. It's an interesting word because there is nothing "cute" about getting hurt.

"So, I can still play basketball with it?"

Dr. Osburn immediately shakes his head. "Oh, no. Even if it's just sprained, you'll need to avoid any kind of exercise for at least a week."

"A week! But I have basketball tryouts next week. I've got to practice."

"Oh, that's great that you're playing a sport . . . but there's no way you'll be able to practice before tryouts."

An hour later, Mom and I get the X-rays taken. Good news. No fracture. Still, Dr. Osburn gives me a finger splint to wear. Mom figures we're done and reaches for her purse.

"Mom?" I turn to her. "Would you mind if I talked with Dr. Osburn by myself?"

"Oh, sure." She hangs her purse over her shoulder. "I'll be outside in the waiting area. Let you *guys* talk."

Dr. Osburn takes a seat and leans back—exactly like he did last year, after Mom asked him if he could have "the talk" with me about the birds and the bees.

"Okay, Marco. What's on your mind?"

"Well," I say, staring down at my feet. "I heard that

you can tell how tall a person will be by looking at an X-ray of their hand."

He nods. "Are you still worried about your size?"

I nod back. "According to California seat belt laws, I should technically be riding in a booster." I look up. "A booster!"

Dr. Osburn reaches back and flips his computer screen so both of us can see it.

"You see these spots here?" He points at some tiny dark spots. "These growing zones are called growth plates. They get smaller as you grow. Eventually disappear."

I can't help but smile. "So I have more growing to do, right?"

Dr. Osburn smiles. "This isn't my area of expertise, but yes, I'd say you have got quite a bit more growing to do."

Without thinking, I jump up and hug him. It only takes a nanosecond before I realize what I've done. But when he hugs me back, I relax and squeeze harder, wondering if my dad would ever do the same.

ISAAC

CHAPTER 19

The smell of steamed corn dogs and mustard hits me. Mostly the mustard. Marco's buddies are busy spreading out their lunches. Strangely, there's no sign of Marco.

Orlando hollers and waves me in. But with Marco not there, I'm not sure I can survive a whole lunch period talking about coding languages. Then again, I don't want to be rude either. So I go over to the table and greet everyone. Orlando tells me about Marco leaving school to see the doctor about his injured finger.

That makes two kids leaving school hurt. I still feel bad about Dos Equis. His ankle was hurt bad. There was no way he's gonna be playing ball anytime soon. Poor kid.

I feel bad for Marco too. Hope *he's* okay. He's like super squeamish—actually fainted the last two times he lost a tooth.

I then excuse myself and tell the guys I'm planning on visiting some old friends from elementary. They smile and wish me a good day. *Total community fish.*

Nick and Ryan each fist-bump me the second they see me.

"Dude, there you are," says Nick with corn dog bits flying. "Hey, guess what . . . you don't have to play point guard anymore. Mr. Chavez says there's some sixth-grade kid with mad handles."

My ears perk up. Playing point guard isn't bad, but I'm more of a shooting guard and love scoring, especially from behind the three-point line.

"Dude's name is Alexxander," he adds, "with two *x*'s."

Two x's? My jaw drops. "You mean, Dos Equis?"

"You know him?"

My head feels like someone just bounced a medicine ball off it. "Yeah, I know him."

Nick's face lights up. "Man, this year's championship is a lock. Three-peat champs . . . I like the sound of that." He holds up his hand for me, only I don't high-five back.

"Dos Equis isn't gonna be playing this year. He hurt his ankle real bad this morning."

Everyone stays quiet for a second.

"That sucks," says Ryan, finally. "Good thing we've got Mugs as a backup."

"Mugs?"

"Yeah. Your buddy's gonna save our season."

"My buddy?"

Nick and Ryan answer at exactly the same time. "Marco."

Marco?

I gesture with my hand. "Little Marco?"

In sync, everyone nods, looking as if they'd planned and practiced ahead of time.

There has to be a good explanation for this. When it comes to basketball, Marco knows about as much as my abuelita. And that's pretty much nothing.

"Why are you guys calling him Mugs?"

Ryan gives me a funny look. "'Cause he's short, like Muggsy Bogues."

"Okay, but what makes you think he can play?"

"Dude, anyone who can hang with you on the court has to be plenty good."

Hang with me? Marco hates any sport that requires

contact. He won't even play basketball online against me.

I open my mouth to tell them the truth, but I stay quiet. I don't know how they ever came up with the idea that Marco can ball, but I don't want to hurt Marco either, not with tryouts only a week away.

That's when the idea hits me. Maybe I can teach him how to shoot. I can have him stand in one spot, draw the double team, then feed him the ball for a wide-open shot.

All I've got to do is work on his shooting. I mean, he's supersmart and determined. A few pointers and practice might be all he needs.

MARCO

CHAPTER 20

I get back home wearing my new finger splint, which makes bending and hurting my finger almost impossible. Normally on days like this, I'd go straight to my computer and start a to-do list, writing down all my homework assignments in order of importance. But today, I decide all that can wait. Instead, I go online and do a search for "*how to be a baller.*" The brace makes it tough to type, but I manage.

Most of the hits are all about wearing expensive watches and music videos. So I adjust my search to "*how to be a good basketball player.*" Finally, a bunch of tutorials come up. I scroll past each one until I find one on shooting.

The guy in the video doesn't seem too tall or athletic,

so I click on his video. He's talking mostly about shooting. About proper arch and ball rotation—same as the majority of the videos I've seen so far. Something Isaac excels at.

I take careful notes with my good hand, doing my best to diagram each of the drills. Only it's not easy.

I've got a lot of work ahead of me and can't let minor roadblocks like my injured finger slow me down. I won't lie: it hurts. I'm not known for handling pain well, but today, the pain somehow keeps me motivated.

I head straight to Isaac's driveway and start my warm-ups. One, two, three, four, five, six, seven, eight, nine shots later, I finally make an actual layup.

The feeling is completely epic!

I take the ball and back up a bit, shooting a perfectly arched shot like the ones in the video, only it just misses the rim. I jump up and down, rejoicing in the fact that I finally got the ball at the same level as the rim. At the rate I'm going, I might be fighting off college recruiters by eighth grade.

I move on to harder, more challenging drills that require dribbling. They're a bit tough to do, but calling out my steps really helps.

One. Two. Jump!

Okay. Now I just need to add the shooting to the jumping. Only that part is a lot harder to do than I thought. But I don't give up.

On the twenty-fourth try, I finally get a good shot off. It doesn't even make it close to the rim, but I'm happy with the progress, especially considering my injured finger, which is throbbing so much that it actually has its own pulse.

I toss the ball beside me, then catch and shoot, just like in the tutorials I watched. Each shot seems to be getting closer to the rim. So, I'm not about to give up now.

Again and again, I repeat the drill.

My finger is aching and looks to have plumped twice in size, but imagining Dad cheering me on from the bleachers keeps me going.

This time, I back up all the way to the three-point line. Analytics has proven the three-point shot to be the most effective shot, so I know I need to master it.

Fortunately, I've got six more days until tryouts. Injured finger or not, I'm not quitting.

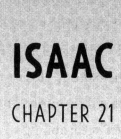

ISAAC
CHAPTER 21

When Amá and I pull into the cul-de-sac, we spot Marco on our driveway . . . practicing his shooting? Guess this whole thing about him playing ball for the school is true.

Amá parks the van along the street. I sit back and watch Marco as he launches air ball after air ball from just beyond the driveway crack I use to mark as the free-throw line.

Each time, he squares up with his knees locked together, double-dribbles twice, and does this head-jerk thing as he shoots that makes him look like a Pez dispenser. No surprise, the ball doesn't even come close to the basket.

"Mijo," Amá says, "I know very little about playing

baloncesto, but I think Marco could use a little help."

A little help? I don't want to say he's bad, but watching him play is like watching a newborn deer trying to walk. I jump out of the car and head right to him. "Hey, Marco, how you doing?"

"Great," he says, shaking my hand. That's when I notice the finger splint.

"Dude, is it broken?"

"Nope, just sprained."

"Bummer. I heard you were thinking about trying out for the basketball team."

He nods. "Yeah, I even got myself the best nickname ever."

"Seriously?" This time I pretend not to know—figure he wants to tell me himself.

"The guys are calling me Mugs. Short for Muggsy Bogues."

"Nice! That guy was amazing! He had some crazy handles."

Marco's eyebrows scrunch up close, something he usually does while struggling to write code.

"It means he can dribble really well," I clarify for him.

Marco's eyebrows go back in place and he's now

smiling again. "I've watched a bunch of highlights of him online. He has this mantra"—he holds up his hands like he's spreading out a banner—"'always believe.' It's going to be my mantra too."

I can't help but notice how purple and swollen his finger looks. "Marco, you can't be playing with your finger like that."

"Well, the doctor said I shouldn't practice with my right hand. He never said I couldn't use my left."

I shake my head. "What if you make it worse?"

"Like the time you dislocated *your* finger last summer and kept playing?"

"That's different, Marco. That was a championship game. Besides, I've gotten used to injuries like those."

"And so will I." He turns his back to me and takes another shot. He gets nothing but air.

Great. I've hurt his feelings. I take a deep breath. "You want a few pointers?"

He doesn't answer. Just stares down at the ball.

"I'm sorry," I say. "I didn't mean it that way."

He looks up at me with glassy eyes, hands me the ball, and pulls out his phone. He shows me a few of his dad's posts. Most are of him happily playing with some other kid—*as if replacing Marco!*

143

Marco's voice cracks. "Sports are all my dad cares about. I thought that . . . maybe if I make the team"—he swallows—"he might actually show up for a change."

My eyes well up—and so does my anger. "Come on, Mugs," I say, handing him back the ball. "We're doing this."

MARCO
CHAPTER 22

Watching all those basketball videos kind of helped. But having Isaac here with me is so much better. He's easier to understand. Plus, he's super patient.

First, he has me pretend to shoot so he can check my form.

Isaac rubs his chin and nods, like he sees what the problem is. "Okay, Marco," he says. "The way you stand affects your balance, and you need to have that at all times—especially while shooting." He bends down and pushes one leg over, so I'm standing wider.

"Your feet need to be at shoulder-width apart. Okay, now try bending your legs." He pats at the back side of my knees. "We need to get some bounce to your shot."

I've got no idea what he means with that last part,

but I bend my knees as low as I can. To be perfectly honest, it feels really weird. Really unnatural.

Isaac backs up as I try again. "Yeah, much better." He hands me the ball. "Okay, now, try shooting with your left hand."

I bend my knees up and down, hoping to get some of that bounce he's talking about. *One. Two.* I take my shot. Well, I try, that is. Sadly, the ball slips out of my hand.

"It's no use," I say. Using my off hand makes it impossible. "Maybe I should just settle for being more like Muggsy Bogues's grandma."

"His grandma?"

"Um, yeah . . . I saw tons of photos of Muggsy and his grandma together."

Isaac holds back a laugh. "Dude, that's not his grandmother. That's his teammate, Larry Johnson, dressed up as a grandmo—" He stops mid-sentence. "That's it! I have an idea."

Next thing I know, I'm standing at the free-throw line swinging the ball between my legs, like little kids do at the bowling alley.

"Rick Barry shot this way, and he was one of the best shooters in NBA history."

I have no idea who this Rick Barry player is, but I'm desperate enough to try it.

"On three," calls out Isaac.

I pump the ball back and forth. "One. Two. Three!"

With momentum built up, I catapult the ball and watch it spiral over the front of the rim and straight into the net!

"Swish!" Isaac jumps up and down.

So do I. It's only one shot, but hey, it's definitely a start.

ISAAC
CHAPTER 23

Always believe. Always believe. You'd think it'd be a pretty easy thing to do, but it's not. Not with Marco's injured finger. Not with the stakes so high.

The good news is that Marco has made six under-hand shots in a row. Six! I know. Guess Rick Barry was onto something. Looking at his stats, underhand shooting just might be the most effective way of shooting. Then again, it's also the most effective way of getting made fun of.

Fortunately, we can totally blame Marco's injury. That way, no one will say a thing. "Dude, you're a machine!" I holler out.

Only Marco is too focused to even hear me. And I

like that about him.

I watch him hit shots seven, eight, and nine before tapping him on the shoulder. "Marco," I say, "how about we try sliding over to the wing?"

Marco hesitates, obviously unsure of where to go. So I point casually, trying to be as encouraging as possible.

Marco nods and runs over before winding up.

One. Two. Three. Four. Five straight misses. Marco holds the ball and stares up at the hoop.

"What's wrong?" I ask.

"I'm not sure. I think it's the angle. I don't have the full rectangle on the back to focus on."

"Try imagining the ball going in. That's what I do. My coach says it eventually becomes muscle memory, which is really, really important."

Marco tries again. And again. And again. But none of his shots come close. I hope his muscles don't remember *this*.

I mean, what do you do with a player who can only make free throws? How on earth is he supposed to get to the free-throw line when that's the only shot he has? The defense would never . . .

That's it! Defense.

We could focus on that. We could make Marco a defensive stopper.

I mean, playing defense doesn't require any ball-handling skills, leaping ability (although it helps . . . a lot!), or shooting form. All it takes is a deep focus, the desire to shut down your opponent at any cost, and a willingness to sacrifice your body—something I'm starting to see in him.

"All right, Marco—I mean, Mugs. Come here."

I take hold of him by the shoulders and steer him in front of me. "I want you to squat down low with one palm up. Like this."

I position him like one of those mannequin figures artists use to sketch.

Marco seems really uncomfortable. "Are you sure about this? It kind of looks like I'm trying to . . . you know, poop."

"Then you're doing it right," I answer back. "Now here's the trick. I need you to follow my chest with yours. If I go to the left, you need to follow me, kind of like we're slow dancing, only fast and without holding hands."

I shift my body from side to side while Marco tries to mirror me. But as I switch direction, Marco trips on his own feet and falls, landing flush on his right hand and smacking down on his finger splint with a loud thud.

"Are you all right?" I ask.

He doesn't answer. Just gets back up, holding his hand.

I look down at his scuffed-up knees, then pan up to his scrunched-up face, and catch him blinking fast.

I ask again, only softer. "Are you okay?"

Again, he doesn't answer. Just squats down to our starting point, ready to go again.

Dang. It's a side of Marco I've never seen before. True Mamba Mentality.

And *that* I can work with.

MARCO

CHAPTER 24

Just my luck. A few seconds into my next drill, and I trip over my own foot. My whole hand bangs hard against the concrete. Isaac calls out to me, asking if I'm all right. I peek down at my finger. It's so black and blue and swollen that it's starting to look like a pregnant grub worm.

I'm not going to lie. It hurts. A lot.

The last time I felt this kind of pain was back in third grade, when I was hurrying to go to the bathroom and accidentally caught part of my privates on my pants zipper. Only this is different. I'm not about to run around in circles, screaming for help.

I'm done with sitting on the sidelines, cheering

everyone else. I am a baller now. A real jock. And I've got to start acting like one.

As much as I'd like to, I don't answer Isaac when he asks me a second time if I'm all right. I can't. There's this clump of pain at the back of my throat.

All I can do is get back in my defensive stance and do my best to blink away the tears.

Isaac now has me sliding from side to side, again and again. The toughest part is not crossing my feet, which is way harder than it sounds. After a few falls, Isaac holds me by the shoulders and guides me through the drill. But instead of working on memorizing the move, all I think about is how lucky I am to have him in my life . . . filling in.

We practice like this for a long while, until he eventually lets go, and I'm able to follow without tripping anymore. For whatever reason, I find sliding from side to side a lot simpler than moving forward.

Isaac stands back, smiling. "Great job, bro!" He claps really hard, which only motivates me even more. "Time to move on. Thing is, learning to dribble would take too long, even without your injured finger. Nuh, we gotta get you to impact the game in other ways."

He motions for me to back up. "Okay, now. Pretend that I'm at the top of the key."

I guess I make a face, because he immediately walks me to the correct spot, smiling like it's no big deal, something I really appreciate.

"That's the free-throw area," he says, pointing to the crack on the court.

I nod back. "Top of the key. Got it."

He continues. "Let's say I'm being defended really tight, and I can't shake my opponent. That's where you come in. I want you to come set a screen for me."

"A screen?"

"Yeah. Pretty much. Your job is to get in the way of the other player, so he can't follow me around."

"And you can bust a three in his face!" I say, repeating something I read online.

Isaac grins widely. "Exactly. Only you need to be careful not to set a moving screen."

"A moving screen?" So much for keeping up with him. "Uh . . . what's that?"

Isaac doesn't even flinch. That's probably the one thing that separates him from every other kid I've ever met. He never judges me. Never makes me feel stupid.

"Pretty much"—Isaac leaps and freezes in place—"you can't be moving once you set the screen."

I stand there, wondering what I should do.

Again, Isaac guides me to where he wants me to go and models. "Now, do a hop forward and freeze." He takes a moment to think. "Okay, this next part is up to you. Some players like to fold their arms over their chests to make themselves wider. Others like to cover their . . . tenders below, so they don't get hit there. It's up to you to decide which is more important."

"Which one is more effective?" I ask.

"Elbows up for sure. That's what I do . . . but only during league games."

"Like this?" I go with my elbows up. I figure getting hit in the groin is a small price to pay for making the team.

"Okay," he says, laughing, "I want you to run up to the leg of the other player and pretend like you're going to pee over his knee."

"Pee? Over his knee?"

"Yeah," he says. "You're not actually gonna do it. It's just so that you get him exactly between your legs, so he's forced to go around you."

"Oh." It doesn't make complete sense to me, but I

give it a try anyway. "Like this?"

"Yes. Perfect. Now I want you to roll back the other way."

"Roll?" I don't see how this will help, but again . . . I do as I'm told. I drop down to the ground and roll over toward the basket, then spring back up to my feet. "Like that?"

Only Isaac doesn't answer. He just stands there, blinking.

ISAAC

CHAPTER 25

I stand there frozen, watching Marco roll around on the ground. Part of me is hoping he'll get up and break out laughing at his own gag. Only I know better. He's not joking. He's got that same smooshed face he gets when he's dead serious—his very own Mamba look.

"Good roll," I say, doing my best not to ruin his newfound confidence. "But I think we're ready for something a bit more advanced."

Marco nods the entire time I go over how a give-and-go works, except that when we try running the play, his feet don't communicate with the rest of him. I try to explain how the side of the pick determines which way he should roll, but he's catching on about as quickly as I did when he tried teaching me to play chess.

Okay, maybe not *that* slow, but still.

Suddenly, the driveway lights flick on as Amá comes running toward us.

"I hate to interrupt your practice, but Abuelita is not feeling well."

"Is she all right?" I ask.

"Sí, mijo. Just a tiny bit light-headed, but I still want a doctor to examine her . . . just in case. Could you call your father and see if he could pick you up? Oh, and make sure you get dinner?"

Marco immediately jumps in. "Isaac's welcome to come to my house. My mom won't mind."

"Well, that would be easier. Then again, your father's been asking to spend more time with you." Amá purses her lips. "How about this? Isaac, you call your dad and see if he's available to get you. If he's not, you can spend the evening at Marco's."

With that said, Amá rushes back inside to get Abuelita while I call Apá. The phone rings a good four times before he eventually answers.

"Hola, mijo," he says in a low voice. "How are you?"

There's something a bit odd in the way he asks. Amá's accent comes out when she's mad; Apá's does the same . . . when he's been drinking. Then again, it's not really fair to jump to conclusions like that.

"I'm doing good, I guess. Only Abuelita isn't feeling well and Amá wants to take her to get checked on. Only she doesn't want to leave me alone and wants to know if you could come get me? She thought maybe the two of us could stop by Don Francisco's and get some burgers."

Apá stays quiet for a sec. It's weird. Nothing like him. I can practically hear him struggling to come up with an excuse. "I don't know. What about your homework?" he says. "Wouldn't you rather do it there, in your own room, on your desk? My apartment is so small."

My heart starts to pound, and I literally feel my pulse in my chest.

You know, Apá, it would be so much easier if you just admitted that you've been drinking and are too drunk to come get me. Of course, I only think those words. I'm really not ready to have this talk with him.

So I let him off easy instead. "Yeah, yeah, for sure," I say instead. "I just called because Amá made me promise I would. You know how overprotective she gets. Besides, Marco already invited me over to his place."

He sounds totally relieved. "All right, I'm going to

let you go so you can get started on that homework. Okay?"

"Okay, Apá. Okay. Bye."

"Adios, mijo." Apá's goodbye is quick. He's obviously in a hurry to get back to what he was doing.

Okay, Apá. Okay. I can't believe I just said that. I mean, it's not okay. *He's* not okay. Apá's drinking seems to be getting worse. Only I can't say a word to Amá about it or she might never let me be around him again.

By the time I make it to Marco's house, he and his mom are setting up at the formal dining table. I offer to help, but Marco's mom has me take a seat.

She walks up and pats my shoulder. "For once, I get to feed you instead."

I pan over to Marco, who is standing behind her, mouthing the word *run* over and over again.

His mom catches him and gives him a side-eye before laughing as well. She turns to me, shaking her head. "Don't you listen to him. I might not be the cook that your mom is, but I do know how to make a few things well." She turns to Marco, holding up a finger, warning him not to open his mouth.

MARCO

CHAPTER 26

Mom has me help her set up at the formal dining table, something we haven't done since Dad left. Guess Mom wants to show Isaac that she's not as bad a cook as I sometimes claim.

She exits to the kitchen and comes back with a full platter of mac 'n' cheese bites. They look really good. So good, I can barely believe my eyes. I pick one up with a napkin and take a careful bite, releasing all sorts of steam from the middle. I stop mid-bite, but not because they're hot. Nope, these mac 'n' cheese bites are as hard as a rock and just as tasty.

"These are"—I force myself to continue with the bite—"really good."

"Oh, I'm so glad to hear that," Mom says. "I was

going to add bacon bits, but then I thought, what would Isaac's mom do? So I went a bit more gourmet and added broccoli and cauliflower instead."

Isaac's doing his best not to laugh, making me want to fling a crunchy bit over at him. Of course, I don't, which is good because these little nuggets could really hurt someone.

For dessert, Mom brings us Ghirardelli dark chocolate mint squares—my favorite. I take a moment to show Isaac my best magic trick. It's just a sleight-of-hand move that requires really quick hands. Mom says I could have a future in magic if I wanted.

After dinner, Isaac and I head over to my room.

I pull out my laptop and claim part of my bed. "Check this out. I made a playlist of basketball videos to watch."

Isaac leans over and peeks at my list. "Marco, you've got over thirty hours' worth of videos. What about your homework?"

"Homework?" It's funny, but I'd forgotten all about it. It's okay, though. It's just a few assignments. Nothing I can't do in an hour or two. I look at the time in the corner of my screen: *7:15 p.m.* "Don't worry, I've got plenty of time."

I click on the playlist. "Here. Tell me what you think."

Isaac scoots beside me and watches as a current high school coach goes over his tips on how to make a school basketball team.

Tip number one: Hustle. Work harder than everyone else.

Tip number two: Play to your strengths. Play *your* game.

Tip number three: Be a great teammate. Support everyone around you.

I turn to Isaac. "These are all things I can do for sure, right?"

Isaac kind of nods. "I don't see why not, *if* we keep practicing."

I think about all the shots I made from the free-throw line, about my defensive stance and my improved footwork. "Yeah," I say. "Definitely."

ISAAC

CHAPTER 27

Marco doesn't seem worried about his homework at all, which is more than I can say about me. Even though the school year's just started, I've got tons of homework to do. I try giving him plenty of hints about how late it's getting and about him having to do *his* homework, only he keeps saying he can do it pretty quickly. Wish I could say the same.

Still, it's not like I can just walk out on him either.

Making the basketball team means everything to him. I've never seen this side of Marco before. The guy can talk your ear off if you get him started on anything related to computer coding or his comic book collection!

The thing is, until now, nothing—and I do mean

nothing—has ever come before him completing his homework.

I hope this whole Muggsy thing isn't a mistake. I mean, Marco is doing all he can, but there's only so much you can learn in a week. Still, I can't imagine what not making the team would do to him.

Marco finally peels his eyes off his laptop to face me. His hair is still clumped together by sweat, and there are smudges of dirt across his face. And yet, his smile is somehow as big as the puffiness under his eyes.

I suggest fast-forwarding through a few of the tutorials, but Marco's not having any of that. Fortunately, Amá comes calling out from my bedroom window, reminding me about bedtime. She's still holding her car keys in her hand, looking exhausted.

I climb back to my room in a hurry to ask about Abuelita. Fortunately, she's fine. She simply forgot to take her blood pressure medicine.

It's strange, but Amá never mentions my homework, probably assumes that's what we were doing this whole time. If only that were the case.

I think about the math pages I have yet to solve, the sports figure I need to research, *and* the science article I need to read and annotate, which is probably why the back of my neck tightens, and the front of my head feels like someone just plopped a huge weight inside.

I jump into bed right after washing up. There's a knock and my door opens. I scoot up against my headboard as Amá enters with a look of pride. "I came in to check on you. I saw you and Marco hard at work. I'm so proud of you."

She leans in to kiss me good night. "Buenas noches, mijo. ¡Te quiero!" There's nothing I can do about it but offer her the top of my forehead.

"I love you too," I say back, following through with a kiss on her cheek.

Amá closes my curtains, turns off my basketball-shaped lamp, and shuts the door behind her.

There's no way I can fail her again, no matter how tired I am. I give her a minute to get down the hall, then search my top dresser drawer for the book light I won last year in a classroom raffle. The light is a bit dim, but lucky for me, it's just enough to work on my homework without Amá knowing.

Total Mamba Time.

MARCO
CHAPTER 28

Who would have thought basketball was so complicated? Putting the ball through a hoop is hard enough, but having five aggressives chasing you, looking to steal the ball, makes it ridiculously scary. That's why I must learn as much as possible from these videos.

If it were up to me, I'd be on Isaac's driveway, practicing my—what did he call it—shutdown defense. But since that's not an option, watching footage is the next best thing. It's the same thing pros do.

Isaac's a true friend. He stayed with me as long as he could, left way after . . . *midnight?*

I reach for my backpack and spread all my homework assignments out on my bed. The problem with having honors classes is that teachers feel the need to assign all sorts of extra busywork.

I log in to Math Conservatory and start my online questions. The first six questions are super quick. It's the frequency table that throws me for a loop. The online tutorial is one click away, but each time I click on the *"help"* option, the program gives me another problem to practice on. The software is designed to help me, but really, it feels like it's just punishing me for not knowing the answer.

It's the first time in—well, ever—that I don't understand something in math. It's like something is wrong with me.

I scour my online textbook for sample problems, but when that doesn't help, I try website after website . . . only I'm not finding anything useful. Middle school math is so much tougher than it was in fifth grade. Maybe I'm just not really as smart as I thought I was.

The idea shakes my confidence and suddenly, I feel my hand beginning to tremble. *Oh no!*

Before I know, my lungs are struggling to get enough air. I do my best not to panic . . . but it's already too late.

Mom's room is just down the hall, and I think about calling out to her, only I can't gather enough breath.

I spot a light coming from Isaac's room. Luckily for me, he is still up too.

ISAAC
CHAPTER 29

I spot Marco climbing in through my window. I'm about to make a joke about him sounding like an injured cat, but immediately I see him struggling. He's not foolin'.

"Marco, you okay?" I ask, rushing over to him, thinking it's something about his finger. But it's not. He's actually struggling to breathe. It's pretty clear he's having one of his anxiety attacks.

I tug at his waistband and pull him in.

"I. Messed. Up. Didn't. Do. My. Homework," he says between breaths.

I'm worried.

I've seen just how bad his anxiety gets. His hands and legs go numb, and his heart feels like it just might pound its way out of his chest. And sometimes . . . he's told me the feeling is so bad, he thinks he might actually die.

Poor Marco. I wrap my arms around him—something that seemed to help last time. When I let go, I try to walk him through his emergency steps. "Come on, Marco. Deep breaths," I say. "Focus on your breathing."

He grabs my wrist and squeezes hard. One of his steps is to close his eyes and visualize the air flowing in and out of him.

"Don't worry," I add. "It's your first missed assignment. Trust me, teachers will just give you a warning. It's fine. No big deal."

Marco does his best to answer, but all he produces is a single tear that squeezes out the corner of his eye.

"Bro . . . listen to me. You're amazing. No one expects you to be perfect. Not me. Not even your mom."

Marco shuts his eyes and manages to catch a breath. "*I* do. It's. All. I'm. Good. At."

"That's not true," I say in as serious a voice as I can, only I'm not sure he hears me. Still, I try. "Marco, you could have grades as bad as me, and I'd still be your friend—you know that. Besides, I hear your mom brag about you all the time. It's usually about what a great person you are—never about your grades."

Marco's hold finally loosens as he leans back. Good. That's a great sign.

"You wanna sleep here?" I ask.

His head bobs up and down.

Thank God. Only it's way late. The best thing he can do now is get some rest. I lift the sheets and watch him curl into a ball beside me. I hold his hand for a while until I hear a snore. Proof he's okay.

I think about lying down and going to sleep too. But I know how much Marco's grades mean to him. Getting a failing grade would probably trigger another attack. And I'm not about to let that happen. Not on my watch.

MARCO

CHAPTER 30

It takes me a moment to figure out where I am. Slowly I start to piece the clues together. My pounding heart, the troubled breathing, yeah, it all comes back to me. I look for Isaac, but he's not in bed. I check the floor . . . nothing.

Isaac's asleep at his desk. I'm not sure why he slept there. I walk over and find . . . my laptop next to him?

What the heck? I'm guessing he went back to my room to get it.

I tap the keyboard to wake up my computer.

I'm still logged on to Math Conservatory. I look closely. My math problems have been completed for me, along with the twenty-three other problems that were added because of the help function being used so much. I check the time stamp: *4:57 a.m.*

No way. There's just no way that anyone could stay up and do that many problems for one stupid answer. There's just no way.

I want to wake him, let him know how truly amazing he is . . . let him know how much he means to me. But considering the fact that it's now five fifteen, I figure he'd rather sleep.

I pull the blanket off the bed and wrap it around him.

"Thank you," I whisper before climbing out the window.

ISAAC

CHAPTER 31

I'm in the middle of a dream, where I'm back at school searching for an unlocked bathroom, when suddenly my alarm goes off, ending the nightmare. I wipe my eyes and turn toward my bed. Only Marco is gone.

I get up and peek out my window. Marco's bedroom light is on but there's no sign of him.

Suddenly, my door springs open. "Good morning." It's Marco, wearing one of Amá's aprons, holding a pair of waffles on a plate.

I jump back. "Wait . . . did you just make breakfast?"

Marco looks over at my desk, at his computer. "It's what friends do, right?"

Oh. Guess he knows. He's being all nice about it too, pretending I didn't wreck his homework. Poor Marco.

His teacher is gonna think he's a moron after all the times I clicked the help option. I hope he doesn't get kicked out of honors math because of me.

Stupid me actually thought I could do his honors math homework for him? I mean, I can barely do my own.

I think about my own missing assignments. About Amá and how hurt she's going to be when she finds out.

I want to answer back with something clever, something to change the subject, only I'm not sure what to say. Seems all I can do is take a seat at the edge of my bed and sniff back my boogers as my nose begins to run.

This time, Marco takes a seat beside *me*. "What's wrong?"

I sniff a few more times, letting myself fall backward onto my bed. "I'm just tired," I say. "Only it's much more than that. I *am* tired—that part is true. Tired of being irresponsible. Of failing all the time."

"Well, for what it's worth, that problem you solved . . . I couldn't solve it myself—totally gave up. Guess I didn't have your determination."

I spring upright, massaging my sore back. I appreciate him trying to make me feel better, only that's not really gonna happen, not while there's my own pile of assignments waiting for me on my desk, untouched.

Determination. Yeah, right. I was supposed to stay up long enough to do them too—only I dropped the ball and fell asleep.

With breakfast taken care of today, compliments of Marco, Amá decides to drop us off at school herself—something that only makes me more anxious. It's not like I can do my homework in front of her. Then again, our school is super strict and likes to hand out missed homework notices for our parents to sign. So really, there's no point trying to keep it from her.

"Amá," I call out.

She lifts her head so that our eyes meet in the rear-view mirror. "I—I"—my words stumble—"thank you for driving us."

Just like that I chicken out.

"Yes, Mrs.—I mean Ms. Anguiano, thank you," Marco chimes in.

"It's my pleasure. It's not every day I have the time. Thank you for the delicious waffles. I might want to hire you to work at my restaurant someday."

Marco laughs.

So does Amá.

I practically leap out of the car the second we enter the drop-off turn. "Bye, Amá," I say, waving at her.

Of course Amá blows me a kiss, which I'm obligated to return.

And of course Marco walks over to her window and says thank you.

"Come on," I say, taking off to the lunch area.

There, I plop my backpack onto an empty table and spread out my assignments. Marco pulls up beside me. "What are you doing?"

"Homework. I fell asleep and didn't finish it."

Marco grips my arm. "No way. Please don't tell me you skipped *your* homework to do mine?"

"Dude, it's no big deal. Everyone's used to me not getting my homework done. *You* not doing yours is a different matter."

"Really. And why is that?"

I take a seat, reach for a pencil, and sort my homework in the order of classes. "Look, dude. I don't have time to argue." I check my phone. *Oh, man. Only fifteen minutes before the bell rings.* "So just leave me alone."

Usually, something like that would cause Marco to

completely deflate. And yet, the insensitiveness of my comment doesn't faze him.

Instead, Marco butt-bumps me aside. "I'll handle math. *You* get started with science."

I look over at him, thinking about what to say. Only he's already blazing through my math problems in total Marco mode. All I can do is try and keep up.

MARCO
CHAPTER 32

I'm not sure if everyone has a best friend like I do. No, not the average "bestie" you pretty much only see and talk to at school. I'm talking best friends who know you inside out. Friends you feel comfortable enough to cry or change in front of, friends so close that they feel more like a brother or sister.

That's what I've got in Isaac.

And I would do anything for him. Just like he'd do for me.

Last night was proof of that. And I can't get over how selfish I was. I was so caught up in trying to be something I'm not that I forgot who I am. What I am good at.

Muggsy Bogues? What was I thinking?

I'm Marco Honeyman. Kid nerd. Perhaps King Kid Nerd.

Anyway, it's about time I start acting like it. And I can start by repaying everything Isaac gave up for me last night.

As time runs out for us, I ask Isaac to create a list online of his assignments and share the file with me while he starts packing up his things.

When the bell rings, I rush myself to the boys' restroom and barricade myself in the last stall. With today being a modified day, I am missing elective classes—mostly stuff I already know. But knowing that still doesn't help me feel better about ditching the class.

Taped to the inside of the stall door is a campaign poster with a horrible cartoon drawing of some guy wearing huge diamond earrings. It reads: DON'T GO NUMBER TWO. VOTE FOR DAVID AND GO NUMBER ONE!

Worst poster idea ever!

I try to set up as best I can, which includes pulling down my pants . . . just in case anyone checks under the door.

Isaac's science assignment isn't too challenging, just a bunch of short questions to prove he was listening in class.

Up next is finishing his math homework. Super-easy stuff. Most of the problems are practically the same. Only, there's so much of it! I don't get how this is supposed to help anyone. It's a shame. Isaac would do fine in my honors class—if he only believed in himself more.

One by one, I work through the assignments until my legs start going numb and get all wobbly from sitting too long. But it's nothing Isaac wouldn't do for me.

ISAAC

CHAPTER 33

The bell rings and my science teacher, Mr. Widén, grabs a handful of parent notification forms to hand out to everyone who didn't complete the online homework. My stomach tightens so much that I feel like I might be sick.

"Mr. Anderson. Mr. Lee. Ms. Quiroz." He goes down the list on his tablet. I wait to hear my name, but it never comes. Mr. Widén goes back to his cabinet and puts the rest of the notices away.

I log in to my account and check my homework. Sure enough, it's done. Turned in . . . five minutes ago?

Wait, what?

My brain *must* be all fogged up from staying up too late. At first, it doesn't make sense. But then everything clears up. There's really only one possible explanation. Marco.

I do my best to focus on today's lesson, something about multicellular organisms and their subway systems or something.

But all I can think about is how to get Marco on the basketball team. Instead of taking notes on what Mr. Widén says, I fold the paper into two parts and start jotting down his strengths and weaknesses.

So far, the strengths side stays blank.

Weaknesses
- Marco is like really short.
- He's got an injured middle finger in a splint.
- He's got two left feet.
- He has no experience playing in a game.
- He can't dribble.
- He can't jump.
- He can't shoot. (Unless it's grandma style and at the free-throw line.)

I draw an arrow, moving that last comment to the strengths column.

Strengths

- He's got the heart of a champion.
- Can't miss from free-throw line (shooting under-hand).
- He's got me to feed him the ball.
- He's the best friend ever!

My mind races. That's it. If I can draw the defenders toward me, force them to double-team me, Marco can go to the free-throw line and wait for me to feed him the ball. He can knock down the shots if no one guards him. The trick is, how do I get his man to come to me?

I start sketching out plays. Dream up all the different pick and rolls and back-door passes I can come up with.

Yeah . . . this could work. It has to.

MARCO

CHAPTER 34

I finish Isaac's homework with about five minutes before my first class ends, which works out for me because I literally cannot walk after sitting so long. No joke. Both my legs feel like they're made of rubber. I'm not sure if this has ever happened to you, but it's got me walking like a newborn deer.

Fortunately, untying my shoes and shaking my legs seems to do the trick because I'm able to wobble my way to math class with Mr. Slaughter, who is easily my favorite teacher so far this school year.

Considering how bad my anxiety got last night, I'm feeling pretty good now. I go inside and take my seat, waiting for class to begin.

Mr. Slaughter looks even smaller when he stands

behind his podium. He pulls out his tablet, projecting last night's homework onto the screen. "Before I start with today's lesson, I'd like to apologize about the most recent homework assignment. Turns out, one of the problems I gave you was really tough . . . so tough, in fact, that it took me all period to figure it out myself."

The entire room exhales all at once.

No wonder I couldn't solve it!

Mr. Slaughter holds up a hand. "The other thing I want to do is take a moment to acknowledge the one student in the entire class who *was* able to solve it."

He walks over to my desk, extending his hand to me. "Marco, I would like to congratulate you. Not just for solving the problem, but for your perseverance."

My perseverance?

I wish I could tell him the truth. Tell him that Isaac is the one who stayed up all night solving it. Only I can't.

All I can do is take Mr. Slaughter's hand and return the firm shake.

Oscar, Jorge, and Orlando all holler and cheer, which only makes me feel worse about the whole thing.

"Twenty-three tries." He highlights the number with his tablet. "*Twenty-three tries*, ladies and gentlemen. That is dedication! That is commitment." He looks right at me. "*That* is amazing!"

Mr. Slaughter reaches into his pocket, pulls out a yellow slip of paper, and hands it to me. "This is a homework pass. It's something new the school is trying this year. It's our version of the golden ticket. It's good for any of your classes. Trust me, the teachers at this school will not be handing them out often."

All eyes are on me as I take the paper.

When I think back to how tired Isaac looked this morning, and about how he chose to do my homework instead of his own, I sink into my seat with shame.

The feeling stays with me throughout Mr. Slaughter's lesson. All I can think about is that "golden" ticket and how it's Isaac who really deserves it.

Only there's no way to come clean without getting him in trouble too. And I can't do that. Not after what he did for me.

Mr. Slaughter walks to the center of the room and looks at me, as if waiting for an answer. Only I have zero idea what the question is.

That's when the front door opens. A girl wearing a white badge enters, holding a red slip. Mr. Slaughter approaches the kid and takes the slip from her. "Mr. Honeyman, it's for you. Mrs. Carey would like to see you."

My stomach sinks. "Mrs. Carey?" I ask, just to make sure my fears are justified.

Mr. Slaughter hands me the note. "Yes, Mrs. Carey, our school principal."

This time the class *ooooohs* as if they know I am in trouble. Which I guess I am.

Just like that, the anxiety returns. Each step gets tougher to make, especially when I get to the stairway. I clutch onto the middle handrail and slide down the steps while focusing on my breathing.

I get to the ground floor and pass the same bathroom where I just spent the last period ditching class. Ditching class. Can you believe that? Me, of all people. Ditching!

What was I thinking?

My next thought is to run back into that same stall and hide out for the rest of the school day. But that would only make things worse.

No. My best bet is to just come clean. To ask for mercy.

Yeah, that's the plan. Maybe Mrs. Carey will take it easy on me and not suspend—*oh, God*. The thought is too much for me to handle.

Deep breath. One. Two. Three seconds. And, exhale.

Deep breath. One. Two. Three seconds. And, exhale.

Okay. My heart's still racing, but at least it stops trying to leap out of my chest. That is, until I think about Isaac. There's no way to come clean without getting him in trouble too. I can't do that. Not after what he did for me.

Here we go again. My heart decides to make a break for it after all, and before I know it, I start hyperventilating. I'm not far from the main office, but the way everything's spinning, I don't think I can make it.

Fortunately for me, a security guard finds me struggling and escorts me inside, where I come across a familiar face.

"Marco . . . is that you?" It's Ms. Ornelas, the best nurse ever! Her voice alone calms me. I can barely believe my luck.

She leads me over to a cushioned table next to her desk and has me take a seat. "¿Estás bien?" She hands me a paper cone full of cold water. "You want to tell me all about it?"

I take a long, long sip, then another.

"Look, Marco. We both know what anxiety does to you. Come on, let's have it."

I take one final sip, then proceed to spill the beans on everything. Ms. Ornelas sits there, patiently listening, touching her heart repeatedly throughout the story.

"Listen, Marco. Just go into Mrs. Carey's office and tell her exactly what you told me. She's really understanding. I'm sure she'll go easy on you. If you want, I could go in with you and tell her what a nice kid you are."

I'm about to accept her offer when a boy with half a swollen face dashes into the room in total panic. "I just got stung by a bee!" He's shaking and in tears. "I'm super allergic!"

Ms. Ornelas reaches for an EpiPen and excuses herself as she and this boy go behind the curtain.

Once again, I'm left feeling guilty inside. That kid has *real* problems. I get myself up and walk over to the principal's office. Mrs. Carey puts down her phone and waves me inside. "Please," she says, "have a seat."

I nod, then sit down directly across from the miniature M&M gumball machine resting at the edge of her desk. It's a great sign. A principal who gives out candy to kids has got to be nice, right?

If what Ms. Ornelas said is true, I have nothing to

worry about. All I need to do is tell the truth and confess everything.

"Wow." She scrolls up and down her computer screen. "You are an amazing student! In fact"—she swivels her chair to face me—"I don't think I've ever seen test scores this high before."

"Thank you," I say back.

She presses her lips flat like she's struggling to read my mind, which of course isn't needed, since I'm more than willing to tell her everything. I just need to find the right words to explain. That's all.

Mrs. Carey eyes me suspiciously. She even leans in closer. "That's why I find it so unusual that you weren't in first period today." She holds up her phone for added effect. "I called Mr. Slaughter right before first period ended. He informed me that a few of your classmates swore that they saw you at the lunch tables just before school."

Uh-oh. Mrs. Carey's look doesn't stop there. Her eyebrows are starting to sink in like Mom's whenever she catches me bringing comic books to the dinner table.

I have no choice but to confess now! Only I start hyperventilating again. "I am . . . so sorry. I spent the entire class period . . . in the bathroom stall."

Deep breath. Deep breath.

"I swear. I didn't think . . . it was going to take that long. I figured . . . I'd only be late . . . a few minutes."

"Oh my," says Ms. Carey, her hard look suddenly vanishing. "It certainly doesn't sound like a pleasant experience."

I think back to the math assignment. "Well . . . it wasn't that it was hard. Not at all. There was just so much of it." I look up at her. "My legs were asleep and everything. I swear, I thought I'd never finish."

Mrs. Carey's eyebrows go right back up, and she's now looking at me as if I just lost a newborn puppy.

"Oh, you poor kid. You don't need to be embarrassed. It's perfectly normal—happens to everyone."

"It does?" I ask.

She nods sympathetically. "Yes. In fact, I'm going to write you a special pass, just in case you need to go back to the restroom during any of your classes."

A pass? Really?

"Oh. Thank you, Mrs. Carey, but that won't be necessary. Trust me, I don't plan on ever doing that again!"

She shakes her head side to side. "You poor dear.

Here, take it anyway, just in case . . . and some candy too. You can have it when you are ready."

Wow. First a pass. Now candy too?

Ms. Ornelas was right. She *is* understanding.

ISAAC

CHAPTER 35

Lunchtime finally comes and everywhere around me, kids rush to beat the long lines. Not me. I'm not even hungry. All I can think about is getting home and taking a nap.

Nick and Ryan are sitting with Marco at what I'm guessing is now our table, sorting through their lunches.

"Hey, guys, what are you doing?"

"Check it out." Ryan's all excited to explain. "Mugs told us about what some of his other friends do with their lunches."

Nick shakes the loose Goldfish crackers from the bottom of his brown paper bag. "Our own food buffet."

Immediately, Marco helps spread the orange fishies over a napkin.

"Oh, okay," I say, reaching into my backpack and pulling out a cucumber salad drowned in lime juice and Tajín powder—my favorite. Everyone at the table freezes.

Ryan's eyes bug out. "Dude, um . . . you're gonna share, right?"

"Of course." I barely manage to push the bowl to the center before everyone starts reaching in with their bare hands. "Guys, I do have a fork, you know."

"One fork between the four of us?" says Nick while licking his fingers. "Dude, that would be gross."

I toss the plastic fork into my backpack, then turn to Marco and catch him looking at me. He reaches for a cucumber with his injury-free hand and slides it along the lime juice sitting at the bottom of the bowl. Only instead of scarfing it up like Nick and Ryan, he hands it over to me.

It's salty, but oh *so* good. Also wakes me up.

Marco's voice starts off a bit squeaky. "I still can't believe you stayed up that late to help me."

I shake my head. "You paid back the favor this morning."

Marco shakes his head. "Nope. It doesn't compare. I was only on the toilet for about an hour. *You* barely slept."

Wait, what? I've no idea what a toilet has to do with any of this.

Only he doesn't explain, just keeps going. "My teacher said that problem was nearly impossible for *him* to solve. Why would you go through so much trouble?"

Even though it shouldn't, Marco's comment catches me off guard. I mean, it's simply what makes him . . . well, Marco.

"Bro . . . I only did what you would've done for me." Just then, I feel Nick and Ryan looking over at us.

Ryan turns to Nick. "Would you stay up all night to do *my* homework?"

Nick makes a face. "No way."

"Yeah, that's what I figured. Anyways, maybe we should be a bit more focused on today's basketball try-outs."

Tryouts? "Wait, what?"

Ryan makes a face. "Um, yeah! Didn't you hear? Tryouts were moved up a week, so coaches have more time to prepare their teams for the tournament."

Marco rests his hand on my shoulder. "Are you going

to be okay trying out? You must be exhausted."

"Nuh, I'm good," I answer back, not quite sure I believe my own words.

Nick plops another cucumber slice into his mouth, but that doesn't keep him from talking. "How 'bout you, Marco? Are you gonna be able to play?"

Marco holds up his finger splint. "It doesn't affect my shot at all. Right, Isaac?"

He's right about that. Not his granny shot, that is.

MARCO

CHAPTER 36

With five minutes until the end-of-school bell, Coach Chavez goes on the school intercom to remind us all about tryouts. I look down at the splint on my finger and remember Dr. Osburn telling me to let it rest for a week.

Wish I could. But I can't. Not if I plan on making the team.

Last night, right before my panic attack, I looked up *"best player ever."* Most people agreed on Michael Jordan. I watched a highlights video and realized I could never be like him. So I searched *"hardest-working player"* instead. Most of the results listed Kobe Bryant.

Now work ethic . . . *that* I could match.

I read this one article where an interviewer asked

him why he insisted on taking every final shot. Kobe admitted that it seemed a bit arrogant, but then he explained how he'd worked harder than anyone else on the court for that same moment. Win or fail, he had put in the work to deserve that shot.

I had to ask myself: Did *I* deserve mine? Did I outwork everyone else?

My mind went to all those late nights hearing Isaac take shot after shot in his driveway. The guy had a basketball attached to him most of the time, sometimes two.

The answer was a hard no. Unlike Isaac, I hadn't put in the hard work. A week ago, I couldn't have named a player, past or present, to save my life. And now, I wanted to show up out of nowhere *and make the team*?

It was a pretty dumb idea from the start.

A million-to-one shot.

Still . . . I can't give up.

I text my mom that I'm going to be staying after school, then tighten the splint over my injured finger and walk toward the PE area.

Injury or no injury, I *will* earn my spot.

ISAAC

CHAPTER 37

I bolt over to the locker room before it can fill up. I've heard about how competitive basketball tryouts can be in middle school, especially now that the whole tournament is played out in one day.

That means I'll have to outplay all the eighth-grade boys who made the team last year. To be honest, it would normally be the kind of challenge I thrive on. Just not today.

After last night, my legs feel heavy, sluggish. All I want to do is lie down on the locker room bench and take a quick nap. Just five minutes. Only that's not really an option.

Instead, I go over to the restroom and splash my face with cold water.

The locker room exit is crowded with incoming ballers—eye-ballers really. Each eyeing and measuring each other up. I scoot along the exit corridor, eventually making it outside to the asphalt courts. All half-dozen courts are already filled with kids shooting around and warming up.

I make my way down the courts, looking for Marco and my friends.

The first couple of courts are filled with kids my size, some of whom still dribble using two hands. Nothing to worry about here.

The next few courts have a mixture of seventh and eighth graders. The kids are lined up doing layups. Only instead of trying to simply loosen up, they're messing around with fancy wraparound shots they can't finish.

No worries here either.

That's when I spot the court at the very end, where Coach is watching. It's definitely a who's who of the school's best players—and that's including this girl named Deni. I've seen her play plenty of times during the summer. Man . . . she's physical and can flat-out hold her own with anyone. And I do mean anyone.

I head on over and check in with the coach. Standing

right next to him is Dos Equis on crutches and a blue foot cast.

"Oh no. It's Isaac!" Coach Chavez says, laughing and pointing to his shoes. "You ain't gonna barf all over these too, right?"

I shake my head and laugh, trying my best to hide my embarrassment.

"Good," says Coach, laughing. "I want you to meet my coaching assistant, Alexxander. I hear people call him Dos Equis."

Dos Equis and I don't say a word.

"He got hurt and won't be able to play this year. But he's here to help out any way he can. He's going to be a huge asset to us this season."

I look over at him, but he just lowers his head, as if embarrassed to see me. "Sorry about the other day. Guess I got what I deserved."

His comment catches both Coach and me by surprise.

Apologizing isn't an easy thing to do. Actually, it's exactly what *I* should be doing.

"I'm sorry too," I say, offering him a fist bump. "Grudges are for dummies, right?"

Dos Equis smiles, returning the gesture.

"Come on," says Coach, looking all confused. "Let me introduce you to our star player."

We stop in front of Byron, just as he readies to touch the ten-foot-high basketball rim. His frosted highlights match the fancy trim of his sneakers. He wipes the bottoms of them after licking his fingertips—a nasty habit ballers sometimes pick up.

A crowd of boys gather around.

Without a single word, he approaches the basket in three huge strides, leaping off both legs. It's like watching a rocket lift off toward space.

Byron grabs the rim, not with one hand, but both, before pulling himself up while bringing up his legs and kicking them wildly into the air.

Coach Chavez turns to me, beaming. "I'm looking for someone who can feed him the ball."

"Are you sure he won't eat it?" I say.

Coach laughs. "Doesn't matter. We've got plenty. Come on, I'll introduce you."

Byron finishes high-fiving the boys around him and heads in our direction.

"Byron, I want you to meet someone." Coach turns to see if anyone is listening. "If all my scouting is correct, this is our new point guard extraordinaire."

He makes a face. "Puke Boy?"

"Well," says Coach, "Puke Boy here is gonna be in charge of feeding you the ball, so I suggest you be"—he holds up air quotes—"'extra chill' with him."

Extra chill? Really? Did he really just say that?

Seems Byron gets the message, though, because he immediately holds up a fist. "What up? Name's Byron," he says, as if we've never met before.

Then again, starting over sounds good too. "I'm Isaac," I say, fist-bumping him.

"Isaac!" I hear my name.

Marco's running over to me with Ryan, Nick, and Saul beside him.

Coach peeks at his clipboard. "Isaac . . . are these your boys?"

"Yes, sir." I slap hands with Ryan. "This is Ryan. He's super quick and impossible to guard."

"'Sup, Coach," he says, deepening his voice.

I point over at Nick and Saul. "These two guys can hit threes all night long." I then turn directly to Byron. "They can really spread the floor for you. Get you all kinds of easy baskets."

Byron looks over at Coach with an approving look while Nick and Ryan glare back at Byron with their chests puffed out.

That's when Marco leans in, offering to shake the coach's hand despite the splint. Still, I introduce him. "And this is . . . Mugs."

Nick jumps in. "He's a defensive stopper. Right, Isaac?"

I freeze, unsure of how to answer. Fortunately, Saul chimes in.

"Yeah," he says. "Even Isaac can't shake him."

Coach turns to me. "Is that right?"

My mind races. I don't want to lie, but I can't exactly say the truth either. "Let's just say that I've never seen anyone play defense like him."

Meanwhile, Byron's got this "you've got to be kidding" face on.

Coach immediately jots down something onto his clipboard. "How are his handles? I could really use a backup point guard."

Everyone looks at me, waiting for an answer.

"He can't really dribble," I say, messing up. "I mean . . . not with his injured finger."

Marco hides his right hand behind his back, but the

206

coach walks directly to him. "Come on, Mugs, let's have a look."

Marco holds his finger up for Coach to look at.

"I don't know. It looks bad." He makes another note.

Instantly, Marco buries his head.

Ryan jumps in again. "It's not broken, though. His doctor says it'll be better in a week."

Coach looks up at Marco for confirmation.

"Yeah, the doctor said I only need to wear the splint for a few days. It's fine, Coach Chavez . . . really." Marco raises his head, locks his welling eyes directly on Coach. "I can just use my left hand instead."

Coach's jaw just about hits the ground. "Wait, you were planning on beating out all these kids"—he gestures to all the courts—"with your off hand?"

Marco nods, sniffing back a few tears, which somehow make him look super tough.

"Whoa. That's a true baller right there." Coach makes a giant circle around Marco's name, then leans in closer to all of us. "Don't worry about it," he whisper-shouts. "If you're half as good as your friends here say you are, you're in."

He turns his attention back to Byron. "Looks like we've finally found the pieces we needed."

"No, sir."

Everyone immediately turns to Ryan.

"I ain't playing with that jerk," he says, pointing his finger directly at Byron.

Nick takes a step forward. "Me neither. Not after what he did to Mugs."

I glance over at Marco, who is looking as uncomfortable as can be.

"What did he do?" Coach and I ask at the same time.

Byron chimes in. "I was just messing 'round, man. No biggie. Right, Mugs?"

Marco nods, but Ryan isn't having it. "You carried him around like a baby and pulled down his shorts in front of a bunch of girls."

I roll my hand into a fist and take a step toward Byron. Only Coach pulls me back. "There will be no need for that."

"But—"

Coach silences me with a look. He sighs and turns to Byron, looking more hurt than angry. "Seriously? Didn't we talk about this last season? And the season before that? Man, I really thought we were done with this kind of behavior." He shakes his head, reaches for a page at the bottom of his clipboard, and waves it at him. "You remember our contract, right?"

Byron lowers his head. Apparently, he does.

"Look, man, I've been coaching at this school since it opened. I've dreamed of winning a championship for a long, long time and really thought this would be the year. But above everything, I am a teacher first." Coach looks sadder than the day I threw up on his shoes. "I'm hoping you remember this day, so that it guides you to make better decisions." He holds his palm up, gesturing for the ball.

Byron huffs and puffs as he hands it over.

"You're off the team," Coach finally adds.

We're all standing around in disbelief.

Byron glares directly at him. Finally, he steps away, heading toward the locker room. "Good luck winning without me!"

Coach drops a giant X over Byron's name. "Well, it looks like I've got a huge spot to fill." He turns to Marco. "I just hope you're worth it."

With that, Coach Chavez blows his whistle hard enough that his shorts drop down a few inches. "Time for tryouts to begin. With only one team this year, there aren't too many spots left. You all have two days to convince me to choose you. Good luck, everyone."

I walk over to Marco and congratulate him. Only Marco doesn't seem happy at all.

MARCO

CHAPTER 38

I just hope you're as good as everyone says you are.
I just hope you're as good as everyone says you are.
I just hope you're as good as everyone says you are.
Coach Chavez's words keep repeating themselves in my mind, especially as I watch the tryouts taking place. Sixth-, seventh-, and eighth-grade kids are all here, each vying for their own spot on the team. Each with his own dream.

I see a heavyset boy struggling to shuffle his feet and stay with the boy dribbling the ball, just like Isaac showed me. I wonder how many videos *he* watched. How many hours of practice *he* put in and why *he* wants to make the team.

For someone who just got what he wanted, I definitely

don't feel too good about it. I need to earn my place on the team. So, when Coach Chavez has everyone stand at the far side of each court, I decide to join in.

He demos how to do wind sprints by actually running the court and pointing out each line we are to touch. Everyone laughs as he bends over, completely winded, showing us all a line of his own—one none of us cares to see.

Finally, he blows his whistle.

I take off in a fury, pumping my arms back and forth so fast, I think they just might appear invisible. When I reach the free-throw line, I skid to a stop and touch the ground . . . something the kids around me don't bother to do.

I finish last in the wind sprints, but Coach Chavez doesn't seem bothered. He probably appreciates my doing them correctly.

Again and again, he has us run. By the second set, I beat two of the boys next to me.

By the fifth set, I pass a dozen or so kids. Probably kids who decided to try out last-minute. Still, Coach Chavez's words still ricochet in my head like a missed shot. *I just hope you're as good as everyone says you are.* On the final run, I clench my hands closed and somehow find a way to pump my arms even faster. With a good dozen kids now behind me, I whisper back. "Not yet."

I don't know if this is normal, but my lungs feel like I just swallowed actual fire. Mercifully, Coach Chavez finally blows his whistle and calls for a water break.

As much as I want water, the fountain is a good football field away. Besides, I think it's air I want more of right now. I take a seat with the older kids beside the chain-link fence. Isaac rushes over. Not only is he one of the few boys still standing, but he's also barely even broken a sweat.

"Marco, you did awesome!" He musses my sweaty hair. "I didn't know you had that in you."

"Yeah, neither did I." I wipe the sweat dripping off my forehead. "I'm just glad it's over."

"Over?" Ryan says, laughing aloud. "Man, Mugs, you funny."

Isaac starts folding back one of his legs and stretches it like it's made of taffy. "Yeah, wind sprints are just the warm-up. It's an easy way of seeing who the real players are." He gestures toward the locker room.

I gulp in air. Twenty-five kids, maybe thirty, are

retreating back inside. You'd think they'd at least show up in shape.

Nick's shaking his head, scoffing, "Man. Some people got no heart."

What did I get myself into? Of all the things I've ever done in my life, wind sprints have got to be the toughest one yet. I can't imagine what else the coach has in mind for us.

There's the whistle. Time to find out.

For fifteen minutes or so, he has everyone doing layups, then something called three-man weaves, which really is like weaving, only with a ball and three boys running down the court. Coach has me sit these out, says he can't afford for me to injure my finger any worse. Thank goodness! Because I need the break.

I also sit out the shooting drills.

The boys out here are amazing! Some of the kids make their first shot after only seven or eight tries.

I'm standing beside Coach, feeling antsy as heck.

He blows his whistle and has the kids line up into two parallel lines. "Look, everyone, I've got enough scorers on the team. What I need now is someone who can guard, who can stay so close to the other team's player that they can tell me what he had for lunch."

Everyone pairs up in twos while Coach Chavez shouts out the instructions. "I want you to zigzag along the court. Just follow the cones." Again, he demos the route. "One partner will be dribbling the ball while the other D's him up by sliding his feet."

He searches our faces. "Who wants to demonstrate?"

I raise my hand, then turn over to Isaac. "It's exactly what we practiced!"

Coach bites his lower lip. "Mugs? You sure? I don't want you getting hurt."

Getting hurt is the least of my worries. "Really, it's fine," I say back. "I can guard him with my off hand."

I don't really know why, but everyone oohs and aahs. Even Coach.

"All right, Mugs," he says, "let's see some of that amazing defense I've heard so much about." He pats my back. "Must be your low center of gravity."

Isaac glances over at me and winks as we both get into position.

"I hope you're all paying attention," Coach Chavez calls. "Isaac and Mugs are gonna demonstrate how it's done. Right, boys?"

Both of us nod in perfect sync.

With the sound of the whistle, Isaac begins his

dribble. He bends down low and begins dribbling the ball faster than I've ever seen anyone do. I'm talking Muggsy Bogues fast. I bend my knees extra low and slide my feet as fast as I can.

We move toward the center of the court, then back to the sideline, totally getting into a groove. Isaac's dribbling is almost hypnotic.

"Come on, Mugs!" calls out someone in the crowd. "Steal the ball!"

With Isaac's training still fresh in my mind, I squat down even lower. Isaac's dribbling might be humming-bird fast, but I do remember his bounce patterns and extend my hand into the path of the ball like he taught me, palm up.

Immediately, I feel the sting of the ball slapping against my fingers, causing the ball to roll out of the court. Everyone erupts into cheers while Isaac chases down the ball like lightning.

I'm not sure what they're cheering for, probably something Isaac did. Something I must've missed. Bet it was really awesome, though.

We continue where we left off. Again, I get into my stance.

A few steps in, I feel contact again. This time,

everyone around us seems to lose it, especially the coach, who's calling for us to continue.

Isaac and I match up a third time. Only this time, I catch the look on his face. Isaac looks mad. I must have forgotten a step or something.

ISAAC

CHAPTER 39

After the second steal, the kids are just about losing their minds.

I don't know what just happened. Maybe it's the lack of sleep or just a fluke . . . but Marco has legit knocked the ball loose from me—twice!

It's surprising that someone so slow running forward can be so quick going sideways. Coach might be right. It might have something to do with his low stance.

This time, I bend my legs more, get extra low, and sway the ball from side to side.

Without hesitation, I bounce the ball between Marco's legs, then return the ball back where I started from.

I regret it the second I do it. It's a jerk move. Something some ballers do to show up their opponents. It's totally uncalled for. Guess my temper got the best of me for a sec.

Only Marco doesn't react . . . like at all. Then all of a sudden, as if his body is on some kind of three-second delay, he pokes the ball away from me as easily as if he's shooing a housefly.

I glance over and watch Coach hooting and pretending to be holding everyone back behind him like NBA players do after massive dunks. As embarrassing as it is to admit, Marco got me. Got the better of me. The best thing I can do is cheer and let him have his moment too. I turn to offer a fist bump, but notice the cheers suddenly go silent and all smiles crumple.

Marco is holding on to the middle finger on his *left* hand, wincing in pain. *Oh no!* So much for his good hand.

Coach has me walk Marco back to the nurse's office. I'm feeling pretty bad about the whole thing. If I hadn't lost my cool, Marco might be okay right now. Same with Dos Equis.

Guess Marco was wrong about me. I might be more of an aggressive than he thought.

After everything he's done for me. After all the hard

work he's put in. I should have been happy for him, cheering like everyone else.

When we get to the office, Ms. Ornelas is nowhere to be found. She's already gone for the day. Fortunately for us, the office manager is nice enough to get ice for us and even offers to call home for Marco. Only he's not having it. He wants to get back to the court and finish with tryouts.

"Mugs—I mean Marco. You do know you made the team, right?"

"Yeah, but I don't want it just handed to me like with the homework pass."

"Handed to you? Dude, you just D'd me up . . . THREE TIMES in a row!"

Marco shrugs, paying more attention to his injured finger. "I just stuck my hand out. Anybody can do that."

I shake my head. "No way. Look, Marco, this last season, I only turned the ball over four times—and that includes playoffs. I'm telling you, you've got some real quick hands there. Besides, you worked your butt off to get here."

Marco purses his lips to the corner of his mouth, pointing toward the PE area. "So did all of those kids out there. Bet a lot of them had dreams of being on the team too."

I gesture for him to show me his finger.

Marco holds up his middle finger as I lean in closer.

"Bro, I can't tell if it's swollen. Can I see the other one?"

Marco now holds both middle fingers up to me. "So, what do you think?"

"Well, right now you definitely look like a typical middle schooler," I say, winking.

Marco laughs. "You really believe I deserve to be on the team?"

"After what you just did out there, you might have a better chance of playing than *me*."

Marco and I get changed and wait at the front of the school for my Apá. It doesn't take long for his pickup truck to turn the corner with sixties rock blaring.

There is no hint of alcohol on Apá—yes!

With that thought out of my mind, I fold the front seat forward and take the bag of ice from Marco so he can crawl up and into the second seat. "Watch out for the finger," I say.

I hand him back the ice after he makes it inside. "Hi, Mr. Castillo," he says, waving. "It's been a while."

"Yes, it has been," says Apá, immediately zeroing in on Marco's newest injury. "What happened?"

"I jammed it while guarding Isaac."

Apá gives me a quick glance, smirking . . . like he already knows the answer. "And how did *that* go?"

"I slapped the ball loose three times."

Apá's eyebrows crash together, and he turns to me, surprised.

There's nothing for me to do but nod.

"Yeah, but slapping the ball away doesn't win games," adds Marco, while somehow managing to fasten his seat belt. "Points do."

Apá adjusts his rearview mirror. "Actually," says Apá, "getting stops can sometimes be just as important . . . maybe more than scoring. Either way, I'm super impressed. I didn't even know you played."

"I just started a week ago. Isaac's been giving me lessons."

Apá tousles my hair. "Looks like the pupil has surpassed the master."

Again, I nod. "Yeah, he even had the kids chanting his name. Right, Mugs?"

"Mugs, huh? That's a good one," says Apá, smiling directly at Marco.

That's when Apá offers to buy us burgers in celebration of Marco's amazing feat. Marco texts his mom for an okay from her.

Of course she says yes.

Marco nods and smiles. Only it doesn't fool me. I know a forced smile when I see one. Poor Marco. He must be in some real pain.

MARCO

CHAPTER 40

I know jealousy is dumb. Mom says I should always focus on *my* blessings, not anyone else's. Only, I can't help it. Not with Isaac's dad looking at him like he's the most important thing in his life. Isaac is *so* lucky.

I doubt Isaac even notices, but he kind of leans in toward his dad when his dad ruffles Isaac's hair. His grin slides over to the side of his mouth, just like his dad's.

Suddenly, my jealousy grows even more when his dad suggests a stop for some burgers. I wish *my* dad would take me out. Then again, knowing my dad, maybe things wouldn't go as well. He'd hate that I still prefer Happy Meals and probably say something mean.

I sit up and pretend I'm enjoying the ride, but thinking

about my own dad feels just about as horrible as one of my anxiety attacks.

Every year, Mom has to call to remind him of my birthday. Even then, the best my dad can do is send me a card with enough money for me "to buy something" I want. What he doesn't realize is that the one thing I do want isn't for sale.

"Marco. Marco." It's Isaac calling me back to earth. "So? You okay stopping for a bite with us?"

It's so ironic that the name Marco is the only thing Dad and I have in common. "Yeah," I say. "I just need to text my mom. I'm sure she won't mind."

With that, Isaac's dad takes us to Don Francisco's, a place with the largest and best-tasting french fries in the world. I order a cheeseburger, plain. Isaac and his dad both order some half-pound monster that fills most of their plates.

Listening to Isaac and his dad talk is so different from my talks with my dad. On the rare times we do speak, my dad asks me about school but only half listens when I start telling him about something new I learned.

When I was younger, I used to make up stories about how many friends I had or how I'd made a winning goal during recess. But eventually, I got tired of the lies.

Isaac and his dad are different. They actually talk. They actually enjoy each other.

Sometimes Isaac's dad tells us about what school was like when he was our age. Tells us all sorts of stories about playing ball in the "hood." My favorite is the one about his whole team going to the park to celebrate a player's birthday. After the last play on the court, they started punching the birthday boy (something I still don't really get), when a group of homies from the area saw and decided to join in—even though they didn't even know the kid!

Isaac's dad gets super enthusiastic, even makes funny faces as he relives the experience aloud. "Yeah, and we were too scared to do anything. We just stood there, wincing with each hit. Fortunately, the homies eventually stopped, even helped my friend back up. Thank God he was okay."

I can't imagine anyone living in a world like that, but Isaac swears that all his dad's stories are true.

True or not, his dad has us laughing so much it's impossible to keep our food in our mouths.

I hate to admit it, but I'm pretty sure I have a closer relationship with Isaac's dad than I do with my own.

"Hey," asks Isaac's dad while wiping a mess of

ketchup and mayonnaise off his face. "If you guys want, I could take you two to the park? I could walk you through a few of the secret plays I used to run as a kid. They worked every single time."

Isaac's face lights up, and I can see why.

Leave it to me to destroy the mood. "I don't know. My finger is really hurting. Besides, I'm sure we've both got tons of homework to do." I feel bad making up excuses to go home. But the truth is, watching Isaac and his dad getting along so well reminds me of what I'm missing in *my* life.

Isaac frowns. "Yeah, Marco's right. I've got a bit of homework to do too."

"Oh, okay. But can I at least buy the two of you some pizza . . . you know, for later? All that studying is sure to make you hungry again. It'll take us thirty minutes, tops."

It's so odd to see a dad who actually wants to spend time with his son. If it were mine, he'd be struggling to come up with excuses to leave.

ISAAC
CHAPTER 41

Apá drops Marco and me at my house with an extra-large pepperoni pizza with pineapple on one half and a two-liter of orange soda. Apá insisted.

There's no way our homework is gonna take that long, but the way I see it, Marco and I can have it cold for breakfast—as long as the pineapple bits stay on Marco's side of the pizza.

I wave goodbye from inside the doorway, feeling kind of bad for Apá. He's looking (and acting) a bit lonely. I know the divorce hasn't been easy for him either. I get that.

Marco and I are organizing ourselves at the dining room table when Abuelita catches a whiff of the pizza.

Just like with Marco, pepperoni and pineapple pizza

is her favorite too. Only she goes to the fridge, pulls out the margarine tub we use to store jalapeños, and stacks them super high over her slice, like a game of Jenga.

Of course, she catches sight of Marco's left hand and insists on wrapping his finger over a coat of arnica before going back to her favorite telenovela, which is ending soon. Poor Marco. Between the wrapping and the splint Abuelita had done, his hands look more like lobster claws. I'm not sure how he's going to type on his keyboard.

Eventually, we get ourselves all set up. Marco's side is arranged like he's getting ready for his very own back-to-school sale. Mine, on the other hand, looks more like a movie theater concession stand.

Social studies homework takes an entire Snickers Bar. Science . . . a bag of Skittles. I offer a few of my snacks to Marco, but each time I do, he just shakes his head and keeps on typing away, one key stroke at a time. I wish I could focus like him.

"Hey, you want some more soda?"

He shakes his head. No surprise. I get up and refill my glass with orange soda and return to the dining area with a slice of pizza. "Hmmm. This pizza is sooo good. Sure you don't want any?"

Marco finally plops his pencil down. "Sure, why not."

The two of us somehow manage to finish our homework as well as the pizza. Afterward, we pull out a chessboard but use it to run basketball plays.

Marco is a sponge and absorbs everything real quick—even starts asking me all sorts of questions about defensive rotations he learned online.

"You know, I have a feeling you'd be a really good player if only you'd played ball when you were little."

Marco gestures at himself. "I *am* little," he says, smiling.

I chuckle. "You know what I mean."

"Yeah, I just wish my dad would be impressed by the other stuff I do."

"I totally get that," I say. Unfortunately for me, basketball seems to be the only thing I do well.

MARCO

CHAPTER 42

Doing homework with Isaac is definitely . . . interesting. I don't think we go ten minutes without talking—well, mostly him. Don't get me wrong, I love hanging out with him, it's just that I like to get my work done first. Him, not so much.

Every so often, Isaac gets up for a snack, even though he has an entire corner market within his reach!

The funny thing is how different he is when talking basketball. It seems like he can stay on topic for days at a time without a break. The boy knows his stuff, a real pro.

I leave Isaac's house after a few hours, just a bit after dark. But I leave feeling like I've spent an entire week at one of those prestigious camps Isaac attends. The game is finally starting to make sense to me. The chessboard really helped. The 1, 2, 3, 4, and 5 number stickers he put on the chess pieces to explain the different positions were pure genius.

I didn't know that each player, each pawn—as Isaac put it—has his own set of jobs and abilities.

My job is gonna be to set picks for everyone else, then get myself to the free-throw line for open shots. That's it.

As Isaac explained, my position doesn't allow me to dribble the ball, drive toward the basket, or shoot from anywhere else. It sounds a bit odd to me, but I'm not about to question him. Like I said, he really knows the game.

He even gave me homework. On top of watching a few videos, he's making sure I RICE my injured fingers. *Rest. Ice. Compression. Elevation.*

Isaac says all my hard work will be for nothing if I don't heal in time for the tournament. The word alone terrifies me. Though I've been to a few of them, I've only watched them from the bleachers. Now that I think about it, I've never actually set foot on the court until recently.

The action is fast and loud. Worse yet, the entire gym smells of armpit. It's hard to imagine myself participating. Speaking of which . . . I take a whiff of my armpit. It smells fine to me. I pull back my T-shirt sleeve, looking for any sign of puberty. Still, *nothing*! Not one meager hair, just *another* bit of lint.

I wipe it away. Not exactly something to brag about.

ISAAC

CHAPTER 43

Early next morning, my door slams open against my bedroom wall, waking me from a dream where I'm searching for a bathroom to use.

I leap up startled, instantly awake.

It's Amá, looking panicked. "It's Apá. He was in a car accident."

I don't say a word.

Neither does Amá. She simply gathers my clothes off the floor and hands them to me. "Here, get dressed."

The car ride is silent. I'm guessing she doesn't know what to say either.

Amá holds my hand as we check in with the lady at the front desk of the hospital. She says she's there to see

Manuel Castillo. Chills run down my spine. Nothing makes sense to me. I just saw Apá a few hours ago. Just had burgers and shared french fries and laughs.

The lady hands Amá and me light blue masks and points us toward something called the ER, which is pretty much a large room divided up by diamond-patterned curtains.

Mom picks up her pace.

Me, I lag behind her, weighed down by fear.

Amá peeks into the room first before leading me in behind her. Apá is lying on the bed, connected to more tubes and wires than I thought was humanly possible. It sounds really wrong to say, but I'm scared to get any closer.

I watch Amá walk up close and whisper something in his ear.

Me? I stand at the corner of the bed, hoping that an alarm clock will go off and wake me from this nightmare. No such luck.

I trace the wires sticking out of his veins and follow them up his arm and neck, ending at some machine humming away.

Amá invites me over beside her, but my legs are frozen. So is the rest of me.

I see the look on Amá's face, a mixture of hurt and sadness. I'm glad she doesn't press me to approach him . . . but at the same time, it makes me feel real bad. What kind of son doesn't go to his father's side?

I finally reach over and rest my hand over his. Just as I feared . . . this is all very real.

MARCO
CHAPTER 44

I leap out of bed at the sound of my alarm. The only thought in my mind is getting back to tryouts and showing off everything Isaac taught me yesterday. I pull my shutters aside. Isaac's light is on and it looks like he's up already.

It might be the weather changing, maybe the birds chirping, but I know today is going to be a great day.

I climb out my window and sneak into his room, ready to surprise him. But when Isaac doesn't return to his room, I head on out to his kitchen. It's dark and empty.

My hollers for him go unanswered. So do the ones for his Amá.

I check the garage. Their white company van is gone.

Finally, Abuelita steps out from her room. She wipes the corners of her eyes with a handkerchief and tells me about the accident. Poor Isaac. I can't imagine what he's going through.

I spend every minute before school calling and texting him. Only he doesn't answer back.

Somehow, I manage to get through my morning classes without sneaking a peek at my phone. But at lunch, I rush over to the restroom stall, which now seems to be my special go-to place.

Sure enough, there's a text from Isaac.

Apá's hurt pretty bad.

I try scrolling down for more information, but that's all there is. My hand shakes as I put my phone away. It's weird for me to admit this, but it's true: Isaac's dad is the closest thing I have to a father.

Ask me about my best father-son moments, and I start blabbing about Isaac's dad, not mine.

My favorite memory is of his dad turning on the sprinklers for Isaac and me, way back when it was still okay for us to run around the front yard in just our underwear. Isaac's dad was always full of fun ideas. This particular one included duct-taping three sets of Slip 'N Slides together and coating them with a layer of

Palmolive soap so we could soar across the front yard easier.

Picturing Isaac's dad in the hospital hits me hard. I start to cry aloud, stuttering between each breath with tears coming down my face. I do my best to hold them back, fearful the crying might trigger my anxiety. But there's no way of forgetting the memories I have of him.

No! It can't be. I mean, look at the size of his truck. Nothing could have hurt him inside *that* thing, right?

I think about the time he found me outside by the curb, alone on my tenth birthday . . . watching the cars race by.

Initially, he didn't say much. Simply parked his lawn mower and walked over to me. He looked down at my Disney pass and just like that . . . seemed to read my mind. "I'm not sure this is the best spot for watching cars," he said. "They zoom by kind of fast. A person could get hurt, don't you think?"

Then he slumped down and took a seat beside me, resting his reassuring hand on my shoulder. "Mijo, you okay?"

In that moment alone, Isaac's dad showed me more love than mine ever did my entire life.

I didn't have the heart . . . or the courage, really, to

tell him that I'd been there for more than an hour with my crumpled Disney pass in my hand, waiting for my dad to pick me up. Mom had warned me about letting myself get too excited about any of his promises, but I didn't listen. I figured my dad would want this latest birthday to be extra special. Thought he might actually remember his Juju-bean. Stupid me.

"Guess I'm not the son he wanted." At the moment, I regretted saying that aloud. But then . . . I would have missed out on Mr. Castillo's response.

"Ay, mijo. Please don't think like that. There's nothing wrong with you. You are one heck of a kid. If your dad can't see that, well, that's his problem, not yours. Seriously, any father would be proud to call you his son. I know I would."

As much as I wanted to leap up and hug the man, I didn't.

I couldn't.

Guess I wasn't ready to completely give up on my dad just yet.

"Well," said Isaac's dad. "I don't have Disney passes . . . but I could take Isaac and you to Chuck E. Cheese for some pizza and video games. How does that sound?"

I took a second to watch a black Camaro race past the two of us. I looked up at Isaac's dad with a smile. "Yes, Mr. Castillo. That would be great."

That's when the end-of-lunch bell rings, pulling me back to reality, back to my bathroom stall. I take a wad of rolled-up toilet paper and wipe my face.

Somehow, I'll need to find a way to make it through the school day. I can't imagine how Isaac must be doing.

ISAAC

CHAPTER 45

Nurse Isabel keeps coming in to check on Apá every so often. She probably feels bad for Amá and me because she offers us an extra chair. I thank her. So does Amá. Only, unlike me, she remains standing at Apá's side.

This last trip, however, Nurse Isabel and Amá step aside and have what my social studies teacher would call a sidebar. It's pretty much when adults, usually lawyers, step away to discuss important details they don't want others to know—in this case, me.

I get up from my chair and rest my head on the upper part of Apá's arm, which also happens to be the only area not covered in wires. *Oh, Apá.* I don't want to put the blame on him. I want to believe it was an accident, but as I shut my eyes and hold my breath, the stench of hard liquor coming from him is impossible to ignore.

If only he hadn't been drinking last night.

If only he hadn't driven.

If only I hadn't brushed him off, then he would have stayed home with Marco and me, sober.

I was wrong not telling Amá everything. I could have told Ms. Ornelas at school too. Sure, Dad would've gotten in trouble, maybe even gone to jail for a bit, but he wouldn't be here, holding on for dear life.

Suddenly, I feel a hand rest on my shoulder. I glance over at the rugged fingers and knotlike knuckles, then up at the police officer now standing at my side.

"I'm sorry, kid" is all he says.

The officer's partner has joined the sidebar with the nurse and Amá. She hands a sheet of paper to Amá, who seems to lose her breath reading it.

I'm not sure what's happening, but I know it's definitely not good. I lean in and give Apá a kiss on his cheek, something I thought I'd outgrown a long time ago.

When the officers leave, Amá suggests we let Apá rest. So we step outside to the tiny waiting room next door. We are barely inside when I start bawling and telling her everything that happened the first day Apá

243

picked me up from school. How he slurred his words, and worse yet, how he swerved his truck. Then I tell her about Apá wanting to spend time with me the day before, and how I blew him off.

Amá wipes away my tears with her fingers. "No, mijo. None of this is your fault. Your Apá has a problem. And this time, it finally caught up with him. It has nothing to do with you."

I look up at Amá and wipe the tears from *her* cheeks. "Apá is gonna be okay, right?" I say, sniffing.

"Sí, mijo," she says. "Claro que sí."

I don't know how much time has passed. Here in the hospital, time is one big blur. All I know is that between calls to the restaurant, Amá has spoken with every nurse who has made the mistake of walking past us.

So far, all I've been able to piece together is that Apá's truck flipped over quite a few times. Fortunately, he was buckled in and alone.

Now a nurse approaches Amá. "Your husband is awake. He's calling for you." She shifts her smile over to me. "And you too, Isaac."

I rush over to his side.

His eyes are puffy and red, much like the rest of his

face. Still, he turns his head in my direction, giving me the tiniest of smiles.

"Mijo," he says, moving his hand in search of mine.

I slide it underneath his, and he squeezes it tight. "Mijo, it's good to see you." Apá's voice breaks and starts to squeak the way mine did earlier this summer. "It all happened so fast. A car jumped into my lane as I was exiting an off-ramp. The last thing I remember is the truck rolling over. I wasn't sure if I'd ever see you again."

Apá closes his eyes and makes a face. It's obvious he's in great pain. He takes a second to focus on his breath. Again, the smell of hard liquor hits me. It smells gross, more like something I might use to clean the toilet than actually drink.

"Apá?"

Apá draws a shorter breath. "Sí, mijo?"

"You promised us you'd stop"—I pause mid-sentence, gathering the courage to finish—"so why did you lie to us?"

Again, Apá winces. I'm not sure if it's due to his accident or to my question.

"Isaac!" Mom tries cutting in, but Apá gestures at her with his hand.

"It's okay, mi reina. Isaac deserves to hear the truth. He is old enough."

I brace myself, unsure if I'm ready to hear from him. "The truth is . . . I have a problem."

He turns to Amá with tear-filled eyes. "I hid it from your Amá and you the best I could—maybe even from myself."

Amá takes a seat beside me.

"Wait!" I immediately lower my voice. "What about yesterday? You took Marco and me out. You weren't drinking then, right?"

Apá struggles to continue. "No, mijo. Not at all. I was scheduled to pick you up. It's the one time I'm strong enough not to drink." He turns toward me. "You see, sometimes it's a lot easier to do things for people you love than it is for yourself. Drinking has a way of hiding who a person is. I didn't feel there was much of me I wanted the world to see." His eyes search for my own. "I never wanted you to see me drinking." His voice breaks completely as tears stream down the sides of his face. "My biggest fear in the world is that you would grow up to be like me."

I swipe my upper lip, keep the mocos from dripping into my mouth.

"Mijo," he continues. "I'm sorry I failed you." His head shifts from me to Amá. "I'm sorry I failed both of you."

Amá reaches over. Her hand now cups both his *and* mine.

"Just know that I plan on making it right. I'm going to get help and make the most of this second chance."

Tears now flood down *my* face. I know it's too much to hope for, but just as I see the look on Amá's face, I can't help but imagine that maybe, just maybe, this might be the second chance for our entire family.

Amá tries talking with me again at dinnertime, after she and I get back from the hospital, but stupid me tells her I'm fine and heads to my room instead. Big mistake.

Truth is . . . I can't stop thinking—I mean worrying—about Apá.

I look at my phone, but the idea of online games makes me cringe. So does cleaning my room or doing homework.

Instead, I go looking for Amá. I find her lying on the living room couch, "watching" a telenovela with the earbuds that Apá connected to the TV before moving out.

She's all but completely asleep. I don't blame her. I'd

take a nap too if I could.

That's when I hear Abuelita's walker scratching somewhere in the kitchen and decide to check on her.

"Hola, Abuelita."

She gives me her usual warm smile as she puts an empty glass in the sink. "Hola . . . mijito." Her short pause tells me she's got something on her mind. "¿Cómo estás?"

My first instinct is to lie to her and tell her everything is fine. But lying takes energy to pull off, and that's something I don't have a lot of right now.

"No sé," I say. Only that's not quite the truth either. Guess the truth requires its own amount of energy too.

Somehow, though, Abuelita can read me like an open book and knows that I am *not* okay.

"Your Apá," she says. "I love him like my own son. Beautiful man. But pobrecito had a tough time dealing with his father's death." She takes her hand off her walker and points a finger at me. "It's hard enough to say goodbye to someone you love . . . your poor Apá did not have the best"—she pauses just long enough to find the right word—"*relationship* with his own father."

Apá had mentioned this occasionally when I got in trouble. Instead of spanking me, he'd tell me about how his Apá would whip him with a leather belt. Said he didn't want that kind of relationship with me. But that was pretty much all I knew about my dad's dad.

Apá once mentioned telling his father that he hated him.

"Yes, Isaac. . . . It hurt your abuelito a lot, but like a pair of tercos, neither of them ever spoke again." Abuelita pats a hand over her heart.

"Your Apá fell apart after his father passed, even started drinking in hopes of forgetting the pain." Again, Abuelita pauses. "Only drinking doesn't work that way. It really only delays the pain and makes it harder to heal."

Abuelita brushes her hand along my cheek. "A veces no hay próxima vez. Tenemos que aprovechar nuestras oportunidades ahorita."

She's completely right. Sometimes, there are no second chances. We need to take our opportunities while we have them.

I reach over and give her a hug. "Abuelita. Te quiero mucho."

Her hand squeezes the back of my shoulder much firmer than I would have expected.

"Yo también, mijito," she says back. "Yo también."

MARCO

CHAPTER 46

Somehow, I make it through the school day. I think about calling Isaac and checking in on him and his Apá. And I also don't want to see Isaac lose his spot on the team.

I send him a quick text, then head on over to the PE area. Coach Chavez needs to know that Isaac isn't playing hooky or taking being on the team lightly.

When I get there, the locker rooms are shut and there's a crowd of mostly boys outside the entrance. Apparently, Coach Chavez has already posted a roster of all the kids who've made the team.

Sure enough, my name is there, sandwiched between *Isaac* and *Deni* in the same huge font. It's a dream come true. Only it's rough not having Isaac here to celebrate.

So is hearing the gripes of the kids who don't find their names.

"Really?" a lanky kid with red hair calls out. "How did that little twerp Marco make the team? I swear, I have poops bigger than him."

I seriously hope not.

Suddenly, I feel a pat on my back. It's Ryan, congratulating me. "Looks like now we can get down to business."

There's a lot I want to say at that moment. But instead, I head to the main court, my eyes on the asphalt under my feet.

Worried about my injured fingers, Coach Chavez doesn't let me do much. I mostly run the field and work on my conditioning and footwork.

When the team takes a water break, I tell them all about Isaac. Of course, I never mention his dad's drinking problem. I wouldn't dare.

Everyone stays quiet at first. But then . . . something inside me stirs. "Basketball isn't about winning or losing," I say. "It's about putting in everything you have inside yourself and sharing it with others, helping them to do the same."

I catch Coach Chavez nodding.

251

"Isaac taught me that." Suddenly, an idea strikes me. "Coach Chavez?" I say. "Isaac taught me a few of his best plays. Would it be okay to share them with the team?"

Coach Chavez smiles. "It never hurts to have options."

ISAAC
CHAPTER 47

It's been two weeks since Apá's accident. Schoolwork has gone okay. Our school is sending out home progress reports this week. So far, I've got no missed home-work—that's a plus. But my grades took a small dip at the end, not exactly what I hoped for—mostly Bs.

Getting As is way tougher than I expected, way harder than playing ball. My old basketball coach used to say that perfect practice makes perfect . . . I need to apply that to schoolwork too.

Still, it's better than I've ever done, so I'm grate-ful . . . especially with Apá finally coming to stay in our spare room last night.

Sure, it's only temporary, until Apá's leg gets better

and he can make it up and down the stairs of his apartment. But still.

Saturday morning, he tried getting up for my school's big basketball tournament, but Amá reminded him of his doctor's orders and marched him back into bed.

I can't imagine how excited Marco must be.

I poke my head outside my window and call out to him. "Hey, you ready for this?"

He's on his chessboard. "Yeah, just going over the plays."

Good for him. He seems pretty calm.

Not me. My hands are all clammy as I take a seat at the edge of my bed, looking up at all the trophies on my dresser. None of them means a thing if I can't help Marco get one of his own.

Without Byron on the team, it's important we start the game strong and build up a huge lead early. According to rumors, he transferred to another school just so he could still be scouted by neighboring high schools. With his size, I can see why high school teams would be fighting over him.

I pull out my pocket notepad and go over my secret plays. The ones where I draw the defender away from

Marco and create the double team. Of course, it will still be up to him to nail those wide-open shots, but I know he can do it—even if it's with that grandma shot of his. His dad is gonna be thrilled!

MARCO

CHAPTER 48

Today is game day! I texted Dad days ago. Longest text of my life. Guess I rambled a bit. But eventually, he did reply, which is awesome.

He even told me how excited he was to see me play! Can you believe it? My. Dad. Is. Coming. To. See. *ME!*

Mom didn't believe it, though. She immediately picked up her phone and locked herself in her room to call and make sure he was coming. I get why she's worried . . . but this time things are different. I'm not asking him to come watch me answer questions on Math Field Day or wait around all day in a hot gym for the results of my Academic Pentathlon team. I'm asking him to watch me play a sport, just like he's always wanted.

All he's got to do is show up and watch his son play

ball. That's like a rite of passage for fathers. There's no way he'd pass this up.

For once in my life, I'm going to make him proud of me.

With Mr. Castillo at Isaac's home recuperating, Mom and I decide to give Isaac a ride to the tournament.

When we get to school, Coach has our newly delivered uniforms spread across a table.

Ryan and Nick are already wearing theirs. I search the numbers. It's a long shot, but I search for Muggsy's number, one. I don't see it anywhere. However, just as I'm about to stop searching, I see Coach Chavez holding up a jersey with the number one on it. I run over and he proudly hands it over to me.

"I thought you might appreciate it," he says, offering me a fist bump.

I'm not sure what the rule about hugging teachers is, but I give Coach Chavez a squeeze.

We all run into the boys' locker room—minus Deni, of course.

The jersey is a bit long and fits me more like one of those nightgowns that old people wear in black-and-white movies, but I tuck it inside my shorts, so it works.

After getting dressed, we head to the gymnasium,

which up to now has only been used as a multipurpose room.

The boys all rush over to the ball rack and start shooting. Not me. I'm frozen in place. I've been inside this gym before—it's where we had our sixth-grade orientation—but for some reason, it now looks bigger, enormous really.

The halfway line on the court looks farther away than ever. That, *and* the number of people packing the gym, sends my nerves a-fluttering.

"Don't worry about it. The nerves go away as soon as the game starts." It's Isaac, holding a ball at his side. "You ready?"

I shake my head as I search the crowd of people entering. "How many games do we need to win to reach the playoffs?"

"Just two," says Isaac. "Then the undefeated teams face off for the championship."

My stomach churns. "So we can't lose at all?"

Isaac nods.

"But Coach Chavez says this year's group is the most undersized team he's ever coached." Which I'm sure has a lot to do with me.

Isaac shrugs, then starts dribbling away. "Yeah, but we're also the best."

"Isaac," I call out, feeling a slight tremble in my voice. "What if I mess up?"

He picks up the ball and turns back to me with all the confidence in the world. "Then you make it up on the next play. . . ."

With that, he goes over and joins the rest of the team.

I rub my hands and check on my fingers. Both feel good as new. That's when I spot Dad taking a seat midcourt, alongside his girlfriend and her son.

Dad made it. He actually came . . . for me!

That's my cue to warm up. I go to the ball rack and pick a ball. More than ever, my hands feel just as rubbery as my legs. Only I'm not about to let my anxiety get the better of me. Not today.

This is it, my chance to finally make Dad proud. I got this!

ISAAC

CHAPTER 49

I slip my earbuds on and start warming up. My first few shots go in, which is a great sign. So is the fact that we'll be playing Vista Verde, aka Vista Nerdy, first. It's a tiny school known more for its amazing mathletes.

I kind of feel bad watching them struggle to make their layups. It's great news for Marco, though. Means he'll get plenty of playing time.

The game starts right away. Seconds after tip-off, we score easily as Ryan makes his first midrange shot from the top of the key.

Then Vista Verde inbounds the ball and we attack with a vicious double team on their point guard. Poor kid just about hands us the ball.

It doesn't take long before the game becomes super lopsided. Coach calls a time-out and pulls out most of the starters. I ask to stay in the game, so I can look after Marco and make sure he only gets the ball at the free-throw line. But Coach points to the 17–0 scoreboard.

He's right. That *is* a ridiculous lead. Even Marco should be able to finish the game.

Coach hands Marco the ball, smiling. "All right, superstar . . . let's see what you can do."

Marco tugs at his shorts and enters the court. I catch Oscar, Jorge, and Orlando doing their best to start a chant.

"Let's go, Muh-ugs!" Clap. Clap. Clap, clap, clap.

The rest of the crowd joins in. His size makes him an instant crowd favorite.

Marco looks back at me. I can see him doing his breathing routine—something he does to fight off his panic attacks. I'm not gonna lie: I'm plenty worried right now and feel my anxiety rising too.

Deni, now our tallest player, wipes the ball dry on her jersey. She then inbounds the ball to Marco, before rushing down to get into her spot at the other end.

Marco catches the ball just fine. Problem is, he just stands there looking for someone to pass it over to.

The crowd is beside itself. So is Coach. He's shouting so loud that he's turning purple. "Dribble, Marco! Dribble!"

To be fair, this is all on me. I never should have told Marco he wasn't allowed to dribble.

Marco looks over at me, confused. I gesture for him to dribble, but all he does is shake his head. Guess it's too much to process all at once.

To his credit, he at least attempts to make a full-court pass. Unfortunately, it goes directly to the other team, who lucks out with an easy layup.

17–2. No big deal.

Again, Deni goes to inbound the ball.

"Dribble, Marco. Dribble." This time he hears me and takes a few steps forward. Aside from looking down at the ball, he does pretty good. I fist-pump the air and start jumping just as . . . he runs straight into the boy guarding him, his forehead smashing flush against the other player's chest.

Marco hits the floor and watches the boy score.

The referee approaches Marco, apparently explaining his call.

17–4.

Coach heads directly to me. "I thought you said he could play."

"He can. Sort of."

I run over to the sideline and start shouting instructions. Marco does his best, but watching me mime plays while dribbling the ball proves too much for him.

17–6.

17–8.

The crowd of mostly parents completely turns on Marco. Man, and I thought *middle school kids* were rude. Now I see where they get it from.

I feel terrible.

Before we know it, our lead has been cut in half. Coach has seen enough and puts in all the starters. We get the lead back pretty easily and the crowd mellows.

Each chance I get, I check on Marco, who's now sitting alone at the far end of the bench wearing a towel over his head.

The game ends 23–10. We all line up and congratulate the other team. The majority of players then rush the player-only snack table.

Not Marco, though. He doesn't budge from his spot on the bench.

I walk over to him. Ryan and Nick stand next to me in support.

"This is my fault, Marco. I'm the one who told you not to dribble."

Marco never bothers to remove the towel covering his head. "I wish you'd told me the real truth . . . that I stink. At least then I could have saved myself the embarrassment."

The three of us take a seat beside him. No one says a word.

MARCO

CHAPTER 50

Why did I invite Dad to come watch me play? What was I thinking? After what just happened, I can't get myself to even look in his direction.

Isaac, Ryan, and Nick each invite me to the snack stand. Only I'm not hungry. I just want to go home and hide underneath my bed.

With the tournament still in play, the referee asks us to leave the bench. We take a seat along the baseline and watch the next teams set up. That's when a huge pair of sneakers stops right in front of me. At first, I think it's Coach Chavez coming to yell at me. Only it's not.

Instantly, I recognize the sarcastic laugh.

I can't believe it. It's Byron, wearing a different school

jersey. I'm guessing *he's* the new highly-talked-about recruit.

Byron grins. "Hope you guys make the playoffs, so I can destroy you."

Isaac ignores him completely. "Come on, guys," he says. "We can watch from the sideline."

When the next game begins, Byron completely dominates the entire game.

Ryan and Nick look at each other nervously.

Instead of wearing my jersey like everyone else on a team, I stay in my undershirt, holding my jersey tight in my hand. At this point, I'm just grateful our coach isn't about to put me back in to play anytime soon.

45–6. That's the final score. Except for one shot, Byron did all the scoring.

Our next game is up. I stay at the edge of the stands, away from the team, while sitting on my jersey.

Isaac is amazing, again. He seems to have mastered every aspect of the game. And yet, the most impressive thing about him is how he never celebrates after hitting a three, no matter how close a defender is in his face. Or when he blows by people and scores on a reverse layup.

Nope. Not him.

The only times he cracks a smile is when he makes a play that finds somebody else open for a shot. And even then, it's like he's celebrating their achievement, not his.

It's easy to see why the team loves playing with him.

The final score is 36–28. A lot closer than we wanted it to be.

Most of the team runs over to Alonzo, one of the last kids to make the team. He's got a huge container of fresh watermelon juice he claims will give us the electrolytes and potassium our bodies need to recharge.

Alonzo takes a monster gulp before handing it over to Deni, who makes a face and stops drinking the second her lips meet the juice. Deni immediately runs to the nearby water fountain and spits it out. "Dude, it's all warm."

He shrugs. "It was cold when I packed it in my backpack last night."

"Why'd you do that?" she asks.

Alonzo rolls his eyes. "Duh, so I wouldn't forget it. Anyway, you want some or not?"

Deni immediately hands it back.

The rest of the team takes turns chugging the juice down—everyone but Isaac, Ryan, Nick, and Deni, who are too busy talking about how to best guard Byron.

As for me, I'm not planning on stepping back on the court—ever!

Still, I appreciate the entire team taking turns trying to cheer me up with stories about horrible games they had. They try convincing me to sit with them on the team bench for the next game, only I refuse. Eventually, we compromise, and I agree to wear my jersey as I cheer.

Except for me, Coach was right about our team being his best yet.

With me sitting on the bench, our team is able to move up to the tournament finals—unfortunately, it's against Byron's team. A man in a tight-fitting suit makes it official over the loudspeaker. The crowd cheers in anticipation.

That's when Coach comes over to the five of us, looking rattled. "Hey, guys . . . any of you seen the rest of our team?" He's right; I haven't seen any of them for a while.

Isaac, Ryan, Nick, Deni, and I get up and search the stands. Nothing.

"You guys better start warming up," says Coach, looking nervous.

Deni crosses her arms and gives Coach a look.

"And girl," he immediately clarifies to her satisfaction.

There will be no warming up for me. I'm never setting foot on a basketball court again. "I'll look around," I say, knowing it's the only way I can be of any real help.

The four players head onto the court, still searching the stands for the rest of the team.

I go inside the locker room and call out to see if anyone's inside.

That's when I hear a groan coming from the restroom and rush over. And then . . . I hear and smell the longest, loudest, most explosive fart of my life.

I check under the stall doors. Sure enough, basketball sneakers fill each and every restroom stall. "Wait, you're *all* in here?" I ask, worried.

"Yeah, I think it was the watermelon water." The voice and classic Kobes belong to Alonzo.

"That stuff made us all sick," adds Seth from a different stall.

Suddenly, it's like the philharmonic of farts! Loud, explosive farts that seem to roll their *r*'s. I wouldn't be surprised if each of the kids was physically being lifted off their seats and into the air.

I pinch my nose. "Are you guys going to be able to play?"

Tanner answers with a long fart. "No, man. There's just no way."

I'm about to ask the rest of the team but stop as everyone else concurs with bazooka sounds of their own.

"I take that as a no."

"Tell Coach we can't play," says Zack.

"But you have to. There's no way the team can win with only four players."

"Yeah, guess that means you're gonna have to play," calls someone mid-grunt.

Me? No way. Four versus five is a huge disadvantage. But so is having me on court. "No! There's absolutely, positively *no way*."

ISAAC
CHAPTER 51

23–21. Somehow our team is only down a basket. Ryan and Nick are handling all the offense. They've been on fire from the three-point line and have kept the game close.

Me, I've been wrestling with Byron for most of the game. He's super tall, with long, lanky arms that almost reach the basket netting without him jumping.

Fortunately for us, Deni and I have been taking turns at center. Of course, she's already called two time-outs to run to the restroom.

With only four of us on the court, there's no way to put any pressure on the other team.

I look over at Marco, but he's still sitting at the end of the bench with his head buried under a towel.

I completely understand. I felt that way last year during fifth-grade awards night, when just about everyone received some kind of recognition for something other than athletics. I wish he'd play, though. Trying to cover Byron and the top of the key is wearing me down big-time.

It doesn't help that the other school's point guard keeps feeding Byron the ball on the inside. Stopping him that close to the basket is impossible. He keeps backing me in and scoring like I'm not even there.

All I can do is remember what Apá taught me and not put my head down. He says it's okay to mess up as long as you hustle and go get the point back. He's right. It's on me to make sure we don't fall further behind.

MARCO

CHAPTER 52

Isaac's dad is sitting on the bench, waving his sweater on the end of one of his crutches while leading a chant of "De-fense! De-fense!"

This game is insane. There's so much back-and-forth scoring, it's hard to keep up with all the action. And yet, my dad is just sitting there with a sour face.

I look up at the score. 65–64. Then over at my teammates.

We might be only a point behind, but each of our players is tired. Exhausted, really.

And yet, somehow, unlike me, *they* refuse to quit.

Isaac does a crossover, then follows up with a beautiful spin move that ends with him getting double-teamed at the corner. The other team is swarming him.

He circles back out, looking for someone to pass to. Only everyone is being guarded too closely.

Isaac splits a double team by bringing the ball behind his back and dribbling it through his legs while squeezing between both players with a hop step! It's a move I didn't even know was possible.

The crowd erupts. Only Isaac doesn't finish the drive. Instead, he hits the ground. The team rushes over, but he manages to get up on his own.

Isaac rushes back on defense . . . of course he does. Even with the noticeable limp.

Enough is enough!

I might not be able to do much, but maybe I can help on defense.

I run over to the coach and ask to go in. He turns to his empty bench and sighs. "Fine. Just don't touch the ball."

I head to the scorekeepers' table and take a knee. My stomach is shaking with nerves. After a missed pass, the ref blows the whistle and waves me in.

Ryan high-fives me and points to the player I'm supposed to guard. He might be the other team's shortest player, but he's still an entire head taller than me.

The crowd goes into a frenzy as I enter. Only not in

a good way. The comments are pretty mean. I glance up at Dad, who is sinking into his shoulders like a giant turtle. But I can't worry about him right now.

"Hey," a voice calls out beside me. "Don't go for his fakes." It's Alexxander. "And watch his spin move . . . it's his favorite."

I nod and do my best to ignore the hissing crowd. After all, it's not them I'm playing for.

Isaac is at center court. His chest heaves up and down. Poor guy can barely stand. I rush to his side and offer to switch places with him.

It's probably just desperation, but he agrees.

I widen my stance and slap my palms against the floor like I once watched Muggsy Bogues do in footage. Suddenly, even my own brain is barking orders. *Keep your feet in front of him! Don't let him get by you!*

For the first time in my life, I feel a bit aggressive.

Byron gets the ball and starts dribbling toward me. I squat down extra low—even for me. He laughs and crosses the ball through his legs, but I keep my chest in front of his. It's like Isaac taught me: *Fakes are for fools.* I'm not biting.

He brings the ball back to his right, then attempts

to blow by me. I swear, it's like the game is suddenly in slow motion. I slide my feet and keep my chest up. His elbow is up, and I see it coming right at me, but I hold my ground just like Isaac would.

The blow to my nose has my whole head ringing. I look up from the hardwood and hear the referee blow his whistle.

"Offensive foul!" is what he calls.

The crowd erupts. Only this time they're not calling for my head. This time, they are actually cheering!

My teammates on the court rush to my side and help me up.

Ryan punches hard on my chest. "Now *that's* how you play defense!"

I run up to the other side of the court and watch Isaac bring the ball up. Even with a bad leg, he dribbles past the first defender with ease, only to run into Byron.

There are less than two minutes left on the clock. I know better than to run and ask for the ball. It's no secret I stink at dribbling.

But that's when Isaac waves me over, pointing at Byron's leg. Suddenly, I know exactly what to do.

I sprint over to Byron and jump directly over his leg as if I'm preparing to mark my territory. He's so focused on Isaac that he doesn't see me and runs right over me.

Again, the referee blows his whistle. "Defensive foul!" He holds a finger up on each hand. "In the penalty. Two shots!"

Byron argues the call as the crowd rises to its feet, cheering.

The players are all marching to the free-throw line. I walk over and stand beside Isaac along the key. He's still fighting to catch his breath, but immediately points me to the free-throw line. "They're in the penalty. Means you get to shoot."

FREE THROWS? ME? I look at him for help.

"Mugs"—he shakes his head—"Marco, you *got* this. I believe in you."

65–64. We're down a point. This could decide the game.

My heart plummets down to my high-tops.

I think about all the practice shots I've taken over the last couple of weeks. There's no difference here, not really. Just more eyes watching. I align my toes along the free-throw line and do my best to imagine myself back on Isaac's driveway.

The entire gym goes silent, minus a few hecklers. I go into my shooting stance. For the last few weeks,

I practiced my underhand shot—practically mastered it. Only I'm not about to try a granny shot now. I've embarrassed myself enough.

Perfectly squared up, I bend my knees, feeling the energy travel from my feet and up my body. *One. Two. Release.* To my own surprise, the ball releases perfectly off my fingertips. I watch it spin and soar through the air. It has just enough lift, just enough distance.

And yet . . . it somehow bounces off to the side.

Most of the crowd moans.

Again, the game slows to a crawl. The referee takes a moment to wipe the ball dry. *I* take a moment to search the crowd. I see Dad looking nervous. Our eyes lock, only he looks away as if in shame.

Then I catch sight of Mom jumping up and down right smack in the middle of the stands, along with both of Isaac's parents—even Isaac's abuelita—each cheering for me at the top of their lungs. "¡A la bio, a la bao, a la bim, bom, bá! Marco, Marco, RA, RA, RA!"

Isaac's family's shouts of encouragement reach me clear as day. It's at that moment that I realize something pretty profound. I've got nothing to prove . . . to anyone.

Even Dad.

And just like that, all my nervous feelings suddenly vanish.

The referee bounces the ball toward me.

I take the ball down between my legs. Yes, granny style! Yes, I know I look like a little kid bowling for the first time. But you know what? I could not care any less.

One. Two. Release!

Again, the ball has plenty of lift, plenty of distance . . . only this time, I'm shooting *my* way. For me.

ISAAC
CHAPTER 53

Unbelievable! Marco just tied the game! HE JUST TIED THE GAME! I've never heard a crowd this loud before. Seriously, EVER!

I scan the crowd for any sign of his dad. He is super easy to find, with him jumping up and down like he's doing. I've never seen his dad this excited about anything Marco's ever done.

Poor Marco. He's worked so hard for a chance to impress his dad. One way or another, we've got to find a way to win this game.

The clock is winding down. Only fifteen seconds left!

Sure enough, Byron decides to bring the ball down himself. I think about how badly he embarrassed

Marco and rush in to guard him myself. Like in a game of chess, Marco runs back to guard *my* guy.

Byron glares directly at me and dribbles hard.

I glare back. There. Is. No. Way. He. Is. Getting. Past. Me.

I body him up and put all my weight against him, only I feel my right knee give up on me. *No! You can't do this to me now. You can't let this guy win. Please!*

My only chance is to swing my arm and go in for one last try at a steal. Only Byron spins around and manages to completely avoid me. I'm beat on the play. Nothing more that I can do but watch the jerk set up for a championship-game-winning shot.

But out of nowhere, Marco jumps out to cut him off at the mid-court. I try to run over to help, but my knee feels like Jell-O and I can barely move.

"D-up, Marco!" I call out.

But Marco isn't hearing me. He's holding his ground directly in front of Byron, literally staring him up.

Byron stops in front of him, no doubt looking to embarrass him again. Only Marco's not backing down in the least. Instead, he actually holds out his hand and delivers a "bring it on" call in front of everyone. The crowd oohs and aahs.

That's when I see what he's doing.

Physically, Byron might be twice Marco's size, but mentally, he's seriously outmatched. You see, the rule book says he has only eight seconds to pass the mid-court line.

He's already wasted two.

Of course, Byron forgets all about the game and goes into his best dribbling exhibition.

Six. Five. Four.

Byron crosses over into a spin move, but Marco's too smart to fall for it. Instead, he fakes going in for a steal—a personal favorite move of mine. *Dang, he learns fast.*

Byron backpedals and starts dribbling behind his back, swinging his body from side to side, smiling. I glance up at the referee. He's down to two fingers, but Byron doesn't notice.

Marco goes in for one last strike, leaping forward and diving for the ball, barely missing it. Byron spins and cackles as he goes around Marco. But instead of getting across the line with his final second, he instead glares down at Marco, looking smug as can be.

That's when the referee blows his whistle. "Eight-second violation" is the official call.

The crowd jumps to its feet. Everyone—and I mean EVERYONE—is chanting Marco's name. Not Mugs, MARCO!

From the sideline, Marco passes the ball to Ryan, who dribbles all the way to the top of the key. Immediately, he gets double-teamed.

The team needs me. I put my weight on my right leg, but it just gives up on me. Coach immediately calls out to me, asking if I'm okay. I give him a nod.

The other team isn't buying it. They see me fall and decide to leave me alone, completely unguarded. Guess they don't think I'm a threat anymore. Big mistake.

They don't know that Marco's dad is watching. They don't know how badly Marco needs this win. And they definitely don't know what I'm willing to do to get it for him.

Nick comes over and sets a screen. Ryan drives in toward the side. That's when Marco runs over and sets a screen of his own. Only Byron runs up and practically smothers him with those gigantic arms of his. Ryan has no choice but to feed the ball back to Marco, who catches the ball in perfect triple-threat position.

His eyes lock with Byron's just as he flicks the ball in my direction.

A perfect no-look pass! Most likely his first ever. A credit to how much work he's put in over the past few weeks.

I lean all my weight against my good leg and receive the ball. There's not much left for me to do but shoot.

It's a shot I've been practicing since I can remember.

Whether it's been with a real ball, rolled-up dirty clothes, or a crumpled piece of paper—it's never really mattered. I've practiced this same countdown every chance I've gotten.

Only today, it's my best friend's happiness that is on the line.

"THREE! TWO!" the crowd calls out.

I shoot the ball. The release feels perfect. So does the rotation.

The ball soars through the air as the final buzzer sounds. The entire gymnasium gasps as everyone watches the ball head on its due course.

Everyone but me. Me, I turn toward my family.

I spot Abuelita up front. She's got one arm up in the air, the other holding on to Apá's shoulder. It makes me realize how lucky I am. As, Bs, Cs—even Ds and Fs—my family is always here to support me.

And in Apá's case, it's against doctor's orders.

There's no way I'm gonna give up on my grades. Not when I finally see how much life is like a game of basketball.

Yeah . . . it pretty much comes down to the hustle we put in.

Win or lose, you gotta keep shooting the ball—because eventually, it *will* go in.

It might even swish at the buzzer.

MARCO

CHAPTER 54

The buzzer has sounded, but the deciding shot is still in the air. Isaac is standing at the far end of the three-point line, doing his best to hold himself up on one leg.

I don't know how he does it.

It's like the boy is made of pure vibranium or something.

Everyone in the gymnasium is holding their breath as the ball lands on the rim and spins around in circles. Little by little, the motion of the ball slows until it hovers just over the front of the rim. Then after a quick hesitation, it falls inward . . . FOR THE WIN!

The entire gymnasium goes nuts! And I mean NUTS!

I knew passing up the final shot was the right thing

to do. My research paid off. I watched players like Michael Jordan and Kobe Bryant give up the final shot. It's a team effort, after all.

We all rush Isaac, flailing our arms and jumping around. Parents come rushing onto the court too. The entire scene is deafening.

Isaac hobbles over and wraps his arms around me. At first, I think it's him giving me a hug. Only, it's not. He's struggling to stand on his own.

It hurts me to see him in pain. Especially knowing he did it for me.

The two of us make it over to the bleachers, where Abuelita is still swaying her arms and hips side to side, dancing.

Isaac heads directly toward her, and I watch the way she hugs and kisses every square inch of his forehead.

My mom finds me and gives me a similar greeting, which, if I'm being honest, I don't mind at all.

"Mijo!" It's Isaac's dad coming over with a limp of his own, leaning in and resting his forehead on Isaac's, father to son.

"You inspire me, son." His voice breaks with emotion. "I promise, I will be a better father."

After a quick wipe of his eyes, Mr. Castillo then comes toward me with a hug and congratulates me on my defense.

That's when I feel a pat on my shoulder. I turn around and find *my* dad standing there with the most satisfied look ever.

"Juju-bean . . . you did me proud today!"

Juju-bean? I haven't heard him call me that in so long that I actually feel my eyes starting to well up. All of me wants to wrap my arms around him and tell him how much his showing up means, only I know that's not the kind of son *he* is looking for.

The best *he* can offer is a firm squeeze on my shoulder.

Dad smiles in approval. Of course he would.

Suddenly, a boy appears.

"Dude, that was amazing!" The boy is standing beside a fake-eyelash-wearing lady. It's his girlfriend's son, the one I've seen so much of in Dad's social media posts.

"Thanks!" I say back with clenched fists, same as Mom when we were first introduced.

* * *

Most of the crowd is now gone, leaving a huge mess behind. The school nurse has plastic-wrapped Isaac's knee with ice. Apparently, his knee is swollen but will be okay.

His mom has invited everyone to come celebrate the win at her restaurant.

When Mom reluctantly invites my dad to join us, Dad exchanges looks with his girlfriend. "Thank you, but we already made reservations at Las Brisas. We're celebrating Angie's birthday today."

There's an uncomfortable silence. Luckily for Dad, Mr. Castillo holds Isaac's abuelita back from leaping at him.

"But, Marco, you are more than welcome to join us. I'm sure they can add another seat to the table."

The invitation hits me hard . . . only not in a good way—not in the way I'd expect. I can already picture us at the restaurant. Dad sitting across from me with his arm around this other woman, while her son and I awkwardly bump elbows.

The last meal I had with Dad wasn't exactly memorable. He's all about sports. Loves the Lakers, Steelers, and Anaheim Ducks. A true aggressive, I guess.

Me, I'm all community and love things like reading and doing puzzles. Dad and I just sat and stared into our menus, even way after we'd ordered.

Even though we were only a few feet apart, we couldn't have been more distant.

He asked me about my coding projects and stuff but kept checking his phone for anything more interesting.

I'm not sure I can stomach another meal like that.

"No, thank you," I finally say. "Maybe next time. Maybe after this year's Robotics Invitational Challenge." Yup, just then, I make the decision to join.

Dad seems surprised . . . and also a bit relieved. "Okay, son."

Son. He says it like he might have forgotten my name. But what hurts more is watching him walk away next to a version of a kid I could never be.

The restaurant music is booming from wall to wall— mostly Mexican tunes I'm not too familiar with. The entire team shows up with their families, including those who drank the watermelon juice. I'm so glad they recovered in time to celebrate our team's win.

So does our coach. So do Oscar, Jorge, and Orlando. Deni, too, sporting a new shiner she received during our last game. Man, she's tough. We were lucky to have her on our team.

It's not long before we are served up steaming chicken fajitas and enchiladas filled with cheese so stretchy it practically reaches the other end of the table.

You know that food is good when everyone is too busy eating to say a word.

Suddenly, one of the waiters enters the room with cold drinks for everyone, including a beer for Isaac's dad—his usual. Fortunately, he doesn't take it. Instead, he reaches for the same mandarin Jarritos everyone else is enjoying.

Yes! I know he's going through a lot, and I'm so proud of him for not giving up. I see where Isaac gets it from.

A bit later, Coach Chavez calls for our attention by clinking his glass with his spoon. He makes a speech about finally winning the district championship and how satisfying it is to do so with such a nice group of kids.

That's when he calls me over and hands me the team trophy. "Marco," he says, "we never would have won without your incredible effort. It was you who willed us to victory."

Everyone in the restaurant cheers and applauds, even strangers.

The trophy is heavy and glistens bright gold as I take hold of it. "Thank you, Coach Chavez. I really appreciate the gesture. But I think there's someone in the room who is much more deserving."

I call Isaac over to the front. "This trophy belongs to you."

Isaac limps up and hugs me. This time, it's a real hug. "You sure about this?" he whispers in my ear.

"Yeah," I say. "I'm good with the ones I have."

Mom calls out for a photo and before we know it, just about every adult is aiming their cell phones at Isaac and me.

To think, even after all he's been through, Isaac continues to stand tall.

We wrap an arm around each other and hold the trophy up high as the phone flashes go off.

For the first time ever, I'm finally feeling taller myself.

ACKNOWLEDGMENTS

First and foremost, I would like to thank my *entire* family. (You know who you are!) You are my strength and motivation to keep writing. I truly have no idea where I'd be without you.

To my wife, my true love and best friend, thank you for embarking on this outlandish endeavor with me. Your company and support means the world to me.

I would like to express my deep and sincere gratitude to my agent, Deborah Warren, for her ongoing encouragement, guidance, and friendship.

I am equally grateful to Rosemary Brosnan, for seeing the potential in me and helping to elevate my work to heights far beyond what I could have ever dreamed. Working under your tutelage has been a true godsend.

Thank you to everyone in the HarperCollins family, especially to the super team of Courtney Stevenson, Jacquelynn Burke, Nicole Moreno, Valerie Shea, Vaishali Nayak, Patty Rosati and her team—you truly are the best at what you do.

I am eternally grateful to the amazing Jay Bendt for creating another amazing cover. It is because of your marvelous work that readers are picking up my books in the first place.

In addition, the completion of this sophomore novel could not have been accomplished without the support and guidance of my amazing critique group, The Tightens. Thank you Jesper Widén, Beverly Plass, Heather Inch-Desuta, Alan Williams, and Sonja Wilbert for your support and honest feedback throughout the years.

I would be remiss to not mention my students, who help keep me current in all things "cool." I learn as much from you as you do from me.

Lastly, I'd like to thank everyone, including all the teachers, parents, librarians, and reviewers who helped champion my first book, *Efrén Divided*, and helped so many children feel seen. I hope this book resonates with you as well.

··· ──────── ···

**Read on for a peek at Ernesto Cisneros's
Pura Belpré–winning debut novel, *Efrén Divided*,
a story about family, friendship, and tearing down
the walls being built between all of us.**

··· ──────── ···

ONE

Once again, Efrén Nava woke up to a chubby paja-maed foot in his face. He squinted at the bright yellow rays peeking in through the broken window blinds and looked to his left. But it wasn't Mía's foot. She was fast asleep, cuddled at the edge of their mattress with the same naked plush doll whose clothes she'd taken off and lost a long time ago.

He looked to his right . . . sure enough, the foot belonged to Max. How Max managed to roll over Efrén during the middle of the night was beyond him. Efrén shook his head and sighed. But then he caught sight of a tiny hole on the right foot of his little brother's flannel onesie. Smiling, Efrén licked the tip of his pinky and gave a wet willy to Max's pudgy toe.

Efrén covered his mouth and stifled his laughter as a sleeping Max pulled away his leg. However, the victory didn't last long. Max spun around in his sleep and planted his other foot in Efrén's face.

There was no way to win. Efrén yawned himself fully awake before turning toward his parents' side of the room. Once again, Apá was gone. No sign of his heavy jacket or scuffed-up work boots by the front door either. It seemed no matter how early Efrén tried getting up, he just couldn't catch Apá getting ready for work.

Amá was the same way and never slept in. Any minute now, she'd wake up, unwrap her blankets, and go right to the kitchen to make breakfast. There was a potful of leftover frijoles from last night's dinner, and that meant she would for sure be making fresh sopes this morning—Efrén's favorite.

But before that, Efrén had something important to do. He lifted Max's leg by the pajamas and got up, careful not to disturb Mía, who now snuggled close to Max.

Efrén stepped over the pair of pint-sized legs and arms blocking his path. He wasn't sure which was worse, sharing a mattress with two kindergartners or sharing the bathroom. Their apartment was really one big room, so the only place he could find peace and quiet was the bathroom.

Efrén looked in the mirror, wincing as he removed the tiny strips of tape pinning his ears back against the sides of his head—an idea he came up with after repeatedly hearing Amá warn the little ones against making funny faces.

"Sus caras se les van a quedar así," she'd say.

Their faces freezing . . . That's exactly what Efrén counted on.

It was only a theory . . . but if it were even slightly true, he guessed the same would apply to his ears. If he could manage to tape back his ears often enough, they too would eventually freeze and finally stop sticking out. All he had to do was make sure they folded in just the right way for a few more weeks and presto! Normal ears that didn't stick out like the knobs on Frankenstein's neck.

After taking care of business, Efrén climbed inside the empty bathtub with a library copy of *There's a Boy in the Girls' Bathroom*, by one of his favorite authors, Louis Sachar. Efrén loved reading books—even when he'd read them before. It was like visiting an old friend.

The main character, Bradley Chalkers, was the best. And it wasn't just that he had a really sweet side to him that his classmates didn't get to see. Nope. The boy was super tough and no matter how rough things got for him, he continued to show up and fight. Like Efrén's best friend, David. Another misunderstood kid.

Some kids at school only saw this white kid who likes to dress flashy and flaunt his latest piece of jewelry. But Efrén knew the real David. The same boy who once took off the sweatshirt he was wearing and donated it for a clothing drive in the neighborhood.

Normally, Efrén would lie in the tub reading and laughing until a stampede of feet came running toward the door. But this morning, his eyelids were extra heavy and the need for sleep was too powerful. He couldn't fight it, not after staying up so late waiting for Amá to return from working overtime hours at the factory.

For the last couple of weeks, there'd been a whole lot of talk, a whole lot of chisme (especially around the laundromat) about various raids and stop points happening around town. Efrén tried not thinking about what he'd seen on the news, all the stories about families being separated, kids put in cages. But that was easier said than done.